Daddy's Little Librarian
Book 1

By

Maren Smith

To Todd, the man I simply cannot
imagine my life without.

Titles by Maren Smith:

Black Light Series:
Unbroken (Black Light: Valentine's Roulette, Book 3)
Shameless (Black Light: Roulette Redux, Book 7)
Fearless (Black Light, Book 10)
Determined (Black Light: Celebrity Roulette, Book 12)

Masters of the Castle Series:
Book 1, Holding Hannah
Book 2, Kaylee's Keeper
Book 3, Saving Sara
Book 4, Sweet Sinclair
Book 5, Chasing Chelsea
Book 6, Owning O
Book 7, Maddy Mine
Book 8, Seducing Sandy
Witness Protection Program Box Set

A Few Other Titles:
B-Flick
The Bride Takes A Cowboy
Build-A-Daddy
Daddy's Little
The Great Prank
Her Consort
Jinxie's Orchids
Life After Rachel
The Locket
The Mountain Man
Something Has To Give
Unexpectedly His

Daddy's Little Librarian
Book 1

by

Maren Smith

Copyright © 2019 by Maren Smith

All rights reserved. No part of this book may be reproduced or transmitted in any form or by any means, electronic or mechanical, including, but not limited to, photocopying or by any information storage and retrieval system, without permission in writing from the author. authormarensmith@yahoo.com

This book is a work of fiction. Names, places, locales, and events are either a product of the author's imagination or are used fictitiously. Any resemblance to actual persons, places, and events are purely coincidental.

Originally published as The Bodyguard. However this version has been completely re-written and expanded. It is almost nothing like the original.

Cover Artist: Allysa Hart at Allycat's Creations
Editor: Maggie Ryan
Formatting: Rayanna Jamison

Chapter One

Scotti came awake in the night with a start. She bolted up in bed, her heart already beating in her throat, half because of her dreams and half because of what she'd just heard. Clutching the blanket with both hands, she listened.

Silence reigned through her small, split-level house. Outside, wind pushed against the roof. Downstairs, the living room clock was ticking.

She'd dreamed it. She must have.

Scared, sick to her stomach, and embarrassed to have let herself become so unsettled over something intangible that she couldn't even remember, she lay back down. Rolling onto her side, she got comfortable on her pillow enough to close her eyes, and that's when she heard it again. The soft, deliberate jostling of the kitchen window downstairs.

She knew that sound, just like she knew exactly which window, because that one had the iffy lock. The one that sometimes came open just by shaking the wooden frame. Having accidentally locked herself out of the house once, she'd discovered that trick while trying to find an unlocked window to crawl back in through. She'd shown that trick to Gopher once, back when they were dating and she still thought he might be The One.

They weren't still dating now, however. And he definitely was not The One.

What he was, was the psycho mistake she wished she'd never made and the man springing the window lock that wouldn't stay secure so he could break into her house.

The lock came undone with a click she could hear, the

rattling stopped, and the window slid open.

Gopher was now in her house.

Grabbing her cellphone off the nightstand, Scotti threw herself off the bed and scrambled under it instead. At the point that she dialed 9-1-1, she could already hear his footsteps coming up the stairs.

"911, what is the nature of your emergency?" said the woman who answered the call.

"He's in my house!" she whispered, panic rising the closer those footsteps brought him down the hall. Slow and measured, and not just him. Now she could hear a low scraping accompanying him as he closed the distance, walking past her Disney princess nightlight—temporarily blocking where the light splashed the ceiling and walls—and straight to her open bedroom door.

Scotti dropped her cheek to the carpet, peeking through the gap between the pink, ruffled bedskirt and the floor.

Tall and lean, dressed all in black from the hood over his head to the gloves on his hands and the boots on his feet, Gopher looked like a shadow as he stood there, frozen in her doorway. A shadow with a knife in his hand, with the tip still gouging a line in the wall where he had scraped. So she would hear it and know he was coming for her.

"He's in your house?" the woman from 911 repeated. Unlike the pure calm, business voice she had used when first she'd answered the phone, now she only sounded annoyed. "Is this Scotlyn Moore again? Honey, you know pranking 911 is a crime, right? Usually it's labeled a class 1 misdemeanor, but this is *eight times* you've done this in the last two months. *Eight* times. For you, they'd be justified in upping this to a felony!"

Gopher stepped into her bedroom, pausing just over the threshold, no doubt taking in her empty bed.

Tears burning her eyes, Scotti covered her mouth. *Please just come.*

"Hello?" the operator drawled.

She didn't dare answer, but watched under the bedskirt as his booted feet circled from the foot of her bed to the side she liked to sleep on. He sat down practically right above her.

"Last time we were in this bed together," Gopher said, "I

had you tied to it."

"Felonies mean you go to jail," the 911 operator continued through the phone.

Closing her eyes, Scotti buried her face in the carpet. She was terrified he could hear her breathing. She was also positive he didn't just suspect she was hiding nearby, but that he knew it.

He certainly sounded like he knew as, shifting on the mattress above her, he said, "Someday soon, babygirl, I'm going to have you in this bed again. Want to guess what we're going to do then?"

Scotti shuddered.

"I hope you're listening carefully," the operator said as the mattress springs squeaked when Gopher stood and braced his knee on the bed. "I'm about to do you the biggest favor you'll ever have."

Scotti flinched, feeling the violence in every punching blow as Gopher brutally stabbed her pillow—her, in absentia—to death.

"I'm not going to do anything," the operator said. "I'm not going to alert the police or log this call."

Gopher's knife slit through both pillowcase and memory foam, broadening his attack, cutting, slashing, and stabbing all down the length of her mattress as well. And Scotti felt every slice of his knife as if he were carving directly into her back.

"Do not call back here again," the operator warned. "If you do, you will go to jail."

Shaking, Scotti held onto her phone long after the line disconnected. Eventually, Gopher stopped stabbing. Sniffing once, he pushed off her ruined bed. She heard the click of the knife as he put it away.

"You're mine until I let you go," he told the room.

There was no relief in watching his boots walk away. He got as far as the open doorway, then paused. Turning back around, he lowered himself to one knee and deliberately bent to look at her under the bed.

"Mine," he repeated, while she burst into tears. "Don't you ever forget that again."

She flinched, scrambling as far away from him as the

dubious protection of the bed would allow when he came close again. But when he lifted the pink skirt, it was only long enough to collect Bat Bear (her favorite Build-A-Bear; a dark blue teddy in a Bat Girl costume) off the dresser and offer it to her under the bed.

She took it, half out of fear, half out of reflex. It was her favorite and he knew that. It was the one she always turned to when she wanted comforting and no one was there to give it. He knew that, too.

"Answer my God damn calls," Gopher told her as she clung to it. This time when he walked away, he didn't stop at the door and he didn't come back.

Scotti stayed where she was, hiding under the bed, hugging Bat Bear to her as tight as she could, until she heard the front door open and close again behind him.

Covering her mouth with both hands now, she burst into tears all over again.

Chapter Two

Pirate Pete's Squid House looked like a fast food restaurant on the outside and the deck of an old wooden ship on the inside. Ropes, buoys, and fishing nets provided a certain, seaside decoration. A giant saltwater aquarium was positioned right at the door of the fenced-in outside play area where it attracted the eyes of the children who happily lost their minds in this place. Above the cash registers, a massive smiling squid in a sailor's outfit spread its multitude of arms out around the walls as if it were inviting everyone who placed an order in for a hug. Another slightly more menacing one was perched in the small hallway off to the right where, as it looked to Kurt Doyle as he waited for his job interview to proceed, it perched on the verge of snagging unwary customers on their way to and from the Buoys and Gulls bathrooms.

Seated at a wooden table meant to look like a cargo crate, covered in a paper tablecloth meant to be colored on, Kurt jiggled his leg up and down and waited for the day to get him. He knew it would happen. He even had a pretty good idea of how it would happen. It was a Monday, after all, and Mondays had never been good to him. Not even when he was a boy.

It was on a Monday when he'd caught his first really good case of the mumps, which had in turn made him too sick to go to his first baseball game with his grandfather. He'd crashed his first car through the window of Jacobson and Meyer's hardware store when he was sixteen on, of course, a really sucky Monday. He'd loved that car.

He'd even kissed his first true love on a Monday. Ordinarily, that might have counted as a good thing if only the object of his ten-year-old affections had returned his tender sentiment instead of punching him squarely in the nose.

And though all that had happened a long, long time ago—before his military days and his scant four years on the force—Mondays were still out to get him. Anymore, they'd even stopped being subtle about it. And already he could tell this particular Monday wasn't planning on being the exception to the standard rule.

He slowly blinked his gunmetal gray eyes at the pimple-faced, peach-fuzz of a goatee-wearing kid sitting at the crate across from him and tried his best not to feel resentful. The kid wore a captain's hat on his head and a stuffed parrot hanging crookedly off his left shoulder and, more importantly, a plastic name tag on his shirt that read Captain Tommy right under the capitalized title of 'SHIFT MANAGER'. Captain Tommy couldn't have been a day over seventeen and here he was, shaking his head as he looked over thirty-two-year-old Kurt's employment application.

Just one more Monday in a long dismal line of the same.

"Wow," Tommy said, flipping the application over to read his work history on the back. "I don't think we've ever had a cop apply at Pirate Pete's before. What'd you do, arrest the boss's daughter?"

Tommy snorted as he laughed, thoroughly enjoying his own joke, and because his door wasn't exactly being beaten down by other employment opportunities, Kurt made a half-hearted attempt to smile back.

"Ha ha," he said, not quite deadpanned but close enough so that it wasn't worth differentiating. "Yeah, that's funny."

Tommy seemed to think so, but obviously he hadn't risen to the ranks of Captain on sense of humor alone. Laying the application aside, he folded his hands on the table and looked at Kurt. "Okay so, this is the thing. Pirate Pete plays favorites for no one. Even though you're" —he glanced sideways at the front of the application again— "older than most of the guys I get working here, you don't have any current restaurant experience, so I can't really start you out as a cook. But we do have a cabin boy position open. That means you'll be clearing tables, fetching silverware and drinks, mopping floors and cleaning the bathrooms at least once an hour. Under no circumstances are you allowed to operate the cash register or the fry machine."

Tommy gave him a stern but friendly 'I-know-it-sucks look', as he said, "There's times when you'll be tempted, but it's for your own safety. The job pays seven-fifty an hour, thirty hours a week, because, you know, nobody but the captain gets full-time benefits in this economy. Now, I know that sucks too, but I've no doubt in my mind that if you apply yourself, with time and dedication, you can eventually rise up through the ranks to become a first-rate swabbie, then maybe a deckhand. In a year or so, if you show you've got the stuff, you might even earn your stripes as first mate. If you're really good, someday" —his reedy voice grew cocky— "you could even be a captain."

"I can hardly wait," Kurt said. *Please, somebody, shoot me.* "When can I start?"

"I like your enthusiasm," Tommy said, picking up his application and flipping it over. He blinked twice as something caught his eye, and his smile slowly faded.

And here it comes. "What?" Kurt said, no longer bothering to hide how tired this whole process was making him.

"Well, it says here..." Captain Tommy cleared his throat. "Uh... under felony convictions... that you, uh..."

"Did two years in Two Rivers Correctional Facility?"

The stuffed parrot fell facedown on the table as Tommy leaned toward him. His eyes were huge. In a hushed voice, he asked, "No shit, dude, are you an ex-con?"

Kurt stifled a sigh. "I've been out ten days."

"That," Tommy exclaimed in hushed reverence, "is the coolest thing I've heard all day. I still have to start you out as a cabin boy, though."

"Can't have you breaking the rules, can we?" Kurt said dryly. Pirates certainly not being known for that.

"Want to start tomorrow, two o'clock?"

"Sounds like a plan." So, yay. He'd finally landed a job. Unfortunately, he was now a thirty-two-year-old 'cabin boy' scrubbing bathrooms at a place called Pirate Pete's Squid House.

Monday struck again.

And yet, when Tommy held out his hand, Kurt obligingly shook it. "Thanks."

"No problem." Standing up, Tommy said, "Now, if you'll

just tell me what size you are, I'll go back and get your uniform, then you can be on your way."

"Uniform?"

At that point, a teenager in tan short-pants, white tights, and the red and white-striped shirt of a sailor walked by to clean off a table. Kurt stared after him a moment, his eyes drifting from the white tights all the way up to the paper squid hat worn at a jaunty angle on the kid's blond head. He closed his eyes for a moment, the pain of it all resonating through him.

Eight years in the military, four years on the police force, one gigantic mistake and a false conviction later, and it all came down to this: a thirty-two-year-old man in short pants, wearing a squid on his head for seven-fifty an hour. And for his own safety, he couldn't even work the fry machine.

"I'm thinking you're a large," his new boss said and headed for the stockroom to fetch a uniform. The circle of hell was now complete. "Welcome aboard," Captain Tommy chirped as he lay the pre-requisite shirt and tights in Kurt's hand. "You're responsible for your own pants. They need to be tan and, you know, pirate-y."

Uniform shirt and new paper squid hat (some assembly required) in hand, his pride in tatters, Kurt headed for the nearest exit. With every step, he comforted himself with the knowledge that he'd probably never run into anyone he knew in a place like this. This was a big town anyway. What were the odds that, after this much time, anyone from his old life would even recognize him?

He pushed open the door and stepped outside into the warm summer sun, and damn near ran smack into Krissy Degrassi. She was a little older—three years almost to the month since she'd framed his ass—and probably out of high school now. She also had a young toddler in her arms, one who looked better dressed and better cared for than Krissy herself seemed to be. Her hair was unbrushed. The thick black goth makeup he was used to seeing on her was absent. And when she jerked back reflexively to keep from plowing into him, not only did he recognize her in a heartbeat, she recognized him.

Her face paled. Jaw dropping, she tightened her grip on her baby.

The restraining order was absolutely still in effect, but this was not his fault.

She backed up first.

New uniform in hand, he slipped past her. If he hurried, he'd look like he was running. He didn't run from anyone, and he sure as hell wasn't going to run from her. So he walked—sauntered even—new uniform in hand and refused to let himself think about her, her kid, or what she'd done to him, because if he did, he'd only get angry and what good would that do?

He could barely feel the warmth of the sun on his shoulders anymore.

God, he hated Mondays.

Chapter Three

"I can't wait to meet your grandson," Scotti told the hunched, silver-haired woman who shuffled up to the checkout register, a stack of books in her arms. "Do you really think he'll take the job?"

Laying her bounty on the counter with both withered hands, Sadie Doyle pushed her glasses up on the bridge of her nose and beamed a confident smile. "Trust me, dear. He'll be perfect for you." Her gray eyes sparkled as she winked. "He's big. He's tough. He's practically fearless, just like his grandfather—God rest him—used to be. Why, just the other day there was this spider—" Sadie spread her hands as wide as her arms would let her.

"Yes, but," Scotti interrupted, not wanting to be rude, but also not wanting to get distracted from the import of the topic at hand. Of all her regulars here at the library, Scotti loved Sadie the most. But that woman was a walking, talking distraction on the best of days. Hell, her distractions got distracted. Ginormous spiders aside, if she didn't get Sadie back on track, heaven only knew how far off topic they'd be five minutes from now, and this was just too important for that.

The butchered pillow and mattress in her bedroom, which she couldn't afford to replace, were proof enough of that.

She was out of time. It was proof of that, too.

"I can't pay much," she reminded the other woman. "That's why no one else will take the job." Well, that and the fact that no one believed her. Gopher was smart. Up until last night, he'd left no evidence of his stalkerish harassment. There was a lot of evidence now though, but when she took pictures of it into the police station this morning, they'd actually accused her of scraping her wall and destroying her bed herself. She huffed a frustrated breath and tried not to feel like she was taking advantage of her friend. Or rather, her friend's grandson. "He'll be risking his life," she heard herself say, while her guilt tightened inside her. "Gopher won't like that I've involved other people, and he isn't just making threats this time."

Smiling, the old woman reached across the desk and fondly cupped her cheek. "Don't worry about the money, dear. Or the Gopher. My Kurt can protect you. And being as how he just got done working for the state, he's temporarily between jobs. He'll be more than happy with anything you throw his way. Believe me, that ex-boyfriend of yours will wish he'd never started all this. Who knows how my darling grandson will deal with it, but I assure you it won't be half as gentle as being picked up by the back legs and dropped off the back deck into the garden."

Scotti opened her mouth, but that mental image stopped her.

"I know." Sadie nodded somberly. "I'd have flushed it down the toilet, too. Although, I'll admit, your particular problem does deserve more than a good ol' fashioned swirly!"

Sadie didn't even know everything, either. Scotti hadn't told her about last night.

Taking her silence for agreement, the old woman punctuated her declaration with a decisive nod and passed over her library card. "He'll be coming to collect me soon. You can meet him now if you want to."

"All right." Not sure what to hope for, Scotti sorted through Sadie's selection of books and logged them as checked out. Stuffing everything in the other woman's tote, she signaled to another librarian that she'd be away from the checkout desk. Not that Sadie needed any help walking. For a little old woman pushing ninety-two, she seemed plenty spry enough to handle her own bookbag. But outside was a far better place to meet her potential new bodyguard, and so long as they stayed near the door and out of sight of anyone who might be spying on her from the parking lot, then they had a better chance of keeping the inevitable conversation that would follow private.

Hopefully, this Kurt fellow was half as rough and tough as Sadie seemed to think he was. Hopefully, she hadn't exaggerated his abilities. Not that it wouldn't be understandable if she had. She was a grandmother. Grandmothers should see their grandkids through rose-colored glasses. It wasn't just a prerogative; it was practically a law. But if she had, if Kurt wasn't the big, tough bodyguard she had said he was, and Gopher found out what she was trying to do—she didn't want to know what would happen next. It would be bad though. She knew that much.

As they passed the watercooler and reached the lobby doors, Sadie leaned into her and whispered, "Try not to slouch, dear. You only have one chance to make a first impression."

Scotti straightened automatically, but even as she did it, it trickled through her head to wonder why it mattered how she was standing if all she was doing was introducing herself to the man she hoped to hire? She glanced at the older woman out of the corner of her eye, hesitant even to ask. "You—you're not playing matchmaker here, are you, Sadie?"

"Absolutely not. Are you sure you wouldn't like to run a quick brush through your hair before he comes?"

Scotti caught herself before she touched her hair. She frowned. "I need a bodyguard, not a romantic complication."

"You're almost thirty now, aren't you?"

"What does *that* have to do with anything?"

Sadie gave her an exaggeratedly innocent blink behind the coke-bottle-eyeglasses that hugely magnified her pale blue eyes. "Why, nothing whatsoever, dear. Why should it?" She then reached up and, before Scotti could stop her, briskly slapped the apples of her cheeks several times. "You really ought to wear a little makeup. You'd be so much cuter, you know."

"Sadie!" Scotti cried, dismayed, but already the hunched older woman had shuffled almost to the main exit. Rubbing her stinging cheeks, Scotti hurried to catch up. "Did you tell him I wanted to talk to him?"

"It's not me who wants to hire him, dear."

"Does he know he's even meeting me?" Scotti's stomach instantly knotted.

"A grandmother doesn't like to get involved."

"Does he know *anything* about *anything*?!"

"A grandmother doesn't like to get involved!"

"Sadie!" Scotti cried, the knots instantly pulling tight enough to strangle, and her heart sinking now too.

Out the door, Sadie went, and Scotti almost followed before she caught herself. The heavy library doors were made of thick wood and glass so darkly tinted that no one on the outside could easily see in. That gave Scotti a slight advantage as she held one door slightly open. She peered down the outside steps, searching what parts of the parking lot that she could see for Gopher's signature Hot-Rod Red Mustang. It was a sunny day. If he was out there, chances were good the top would be down and he'd be in plain sight. Possibly eating an apple, which would give him a reason to have his knife out where she could see it, and remember.

Scotti swallowed hard. She studied every car that she could see, but she didn't recognize any of them. Nor did she see anyone loitering suspiciously.

"I don't see him yet," Sadie said, shuffling out as far as the top of the library steps. She paused to search the full lot, even the parts that Scotti couldn't see from just inside the entryway, and then she came shuffling back. "Maybe we should come up with some sort of secret code before he gets here. You know, on the off chance that he's not what you're looking for."

So no one's feelings would get hurt if Sadie's grandson turned out to be less like Arnold Schwarzenegger and more like Woody Allen. "Good idea," Scotti agreed, a little relieved. She never liked hurting anyone's feelings.

Sadie straightened with an excited clap. "I've got one! How about 'The pig is in the poke'?"

Scotti couldn't begin to see how that might be unobtrusively worked into normal conversation. "What about 'nice car'?"

"Oh, he doesn't have a car yet," Sadie said. "He hasn't had a chance to buy one since the government, uh... released him from his responsibilities. Do you like egg rolls?"

Scotti shrugged with her eyebrows. "I don't know. Depends on who makes them. Why?"

"No, no, dear. I mean that can be our secret code."

"Oh." She brightened. "That might work. After we meet and I've had a chance to feel him out a bit, you could invite me home for egg rolls, and I'll say yes if I want to hire him or no if I don't."

Sadie tsked. "Well, that won't work. I never cook Chinese, and Kurt knows that."

"We've got to think of—" Scotti began, but Sadie suddenly threw up her hands.

"Shh!" the old woman loudly shushed her. "Here he comes! Here he comes!"

Had Scotti been any shorter, she'd have been tackled to the ground in Sadie's exuberant attempts to smooth down her hair and pinch more color into her cheeks.

"Ouch! Stop it!" But Scotti's protests were cut abruptly short when the old woman spun her around and gave her a sharp push, straight out the door into the shadow of the library porch, and quite literally into the startled embrace of one of the most handsome men Scotti had ever had the good fortune to fall into. She didn't even mind that he was soaking wet from head to toe. His red and black flannel shirt fit him like a second skin, so did his dark blue jeans. The man could have been a clothing model, or a body builder, or Arnold Schwarzenegger's personal stunt double, from the shoulders down. His physique more than made up for any secondhand wetness now soaking into the front of her business dress.

He had steel-gray eyes and jet-black hair, buzzed militarily short against his scalp. He had a mouth so delicious that it would have made a nun reconsider, and a hard, square, mess-with-me-buster-and-I'll-clean-your-clock jawline, the overall effect of which was only slightly gentled by the dimple that kissed his chin.

He looked big. He looked strong.

He looked like he ought to be somebody's Daddy, Scotti's Little voice whispered inside her head. *Somebody like me would be nice.*

"This," she vaguely heard Sadie say from somewhere behind her, "is my grandson."

Scotti sighed, melting in his arms as she gazed up into Kurt Doyle's handsome gray eyes. "Egg rolls," she said. "I'll take two, please."

* * * * *

Kurt didn't think it possible for the day to get any worse, but Monday quickly proved him wrong.

He'd spent most of the walk to the library fiddling with the squid hat, trying to put it together. Fold out Flap A, insert Tab B into Flap G and secure with Tab C. Tab C? Where the hell was C?

By the time he was within a few blocks of the library, he'd come to the conclusion that he didn't deserve the added responsibilities of operating a French fry machine. In fact, it was a wonder he was allowed to leave the house without supervision.

And then he ran into the bees. Or rather, he ran into the post that they called home and accidentally knocked the bottom half of the nest loose from the rear of the sign, sending it crashing to the sidewalk at his feet.

The bees got pissed.

Kurt ran a block and a half before hopping a hotel fence and leaping into their nearly empty swimming pool. There was just enough water in the deep end to submerge himself if he lay flat on his back with his toes pressed toward the ground.

After ten minutes of trying to catch him whenever he came up for air, the bees finally gave up. Eventually, they went away, and Kurt crawled out of the pool. Not only was he now dripping wet, but he'd lost his paper hat and his stomach throbbed where one lucky bee had got him.

And now, he had a crazy blonde librarian wrapped in his arms.

"Sorry," he said, propping her back up on her own feet. "I don't have any egg rolls on me." He leaned around her, reaching for his grandmother's bookbag and slinging it over his shoulder. "Ready to go?"

Sadie knuckled her fists into her round hips and scolded, "Kurtis Bartholomew Doyle! You mind your manners, mister, and talk to Scotti."

"Who's Scotti?"

The librarian raised her hand. Sure enough, the nametag on the front of her demure white blouse did indeed read: *Hello!*

My name is Scotti.

Great, Grams is matchmaking.

Kurt managed not to groan as he dutifully raised his gaze back from her chest to her eyes. The way his Monday was going, he supposed he ought to be grateful she didn't think he was ogling her boobs.

"Hi. Sorry." When he gestured at her, she dutifully looked down at the spots of wetness soaking into her. Particularly her breasts and stomach, and around her to her back where his arm had hugged her and his sleeve had shared the wetness. "Sorry about that. I fell in a pool."

"A pool?" Plucking at her blouse, she fluffed it in and out, as if that might help dry it faster.

"In my defense, I was being chased."

Dismay shadowed her face. "Chased? Did he have a knife?"

"It wasn't a 'he'," he said, the cop in him perking his ears. "It was more of a 'them', and why did you just say that like you thought you knew who would be chasing me?"

She tapped her fingers, dismay only growing. "Them? He has... a gang now?"

He stood six-foot-four to her five-foot-one (maybe). When he drew himself up to his full, impressive height and folded his arms across his chest, he knew she noticed. "Okay, I was talking about bees. What, or who, are you talking about?"

She went from tapping her fingers to twisting them and didn't answer.

He looked from her to his grandmother. "All right, what's going on?"

"This," Sadie said, "is a conversation best had in private." Planting a hand to each of their backs, the old woman pushed until they started moving, and she shooed them back into the library and all the way down the foyer toward the bathrooms.

"Grams," he warned, in his most authoritative tone, but she still shoved him into the nearest bathroom.

"Give us a moment, dear," the old woman told Scotti, just before shutting the door, sealing them into the bathroom together. Before he could say a word, she rounded on him like the grumpy, old, Coke-bottle-glasses-wearing honey badger, who used to make him cookies after school. "You be nice to this girl, young man. You be nice to her or so help me—" She didn't finish her threat, but she did stab at him with her finger, letting him know without a doubt how serious she was.

"Oh, for fu—"

"No swearing!" She smacked his arm.

He glowered; she bloomed into an unbelievably innocent smile and swung the bathroom door open again.

"Oh, dear!" she called, and swept back out again. "Your turn. He can't wait to talk to you."

"Oh for—" Rubbing his face, Kurt censored himself a half second before the shell-shocked blonde was pushed into the men's room with him.

"I'll be the lookout," Sadie mock whispered and yanked the door firmly shut. No doubt, she'd have her back shoved up against it, making sure the two of them were good and alone for who knew how long, and for who knew what for.

"Welcome to hell," he said dryly. "What are you in for?"

"In for?" The little blonde stood frozen when she'd been shoved, her brown eyes huge, her fingers tapping worriedly. "I don't know, but I have a funny feeling we're being set up."

She looked confused, apologetic and not at all like she was in on whatever manipulation his wily grandmother was conjuring.

Kurt softened slightly. "We are." He started to fold his arms, but stopped when he felt the telltale pinch of a stinger still embedded in his side and catching against his shirt. He started to lift his shirt, then stopped when he realized she was watching. Her cheeks were flushed, but her eyes were wide. Unlike that minute attraction when she'd first fallen into his arms, right now she honestly seemed upset. "You might want to…" He motioned for her to turn around.

"I don't think she'll let me leave," the librarian whispered after glancing at the door.

He almost laughed. She definitely wasn't in on the manipulation. "No, she won't. Don't let the frail shuffle fool you. That woman is a force of nature."

He'd given her the option. If she wasn't going to turn around, then he wasn't going to be embarrassed about it, either.

Hiking his shirt, Kurt angled his side toward the mirror and tried to feel for where the stinger was. The sink was high and the mirror was higher, making it impossible for him to see the tiny thing. It was also around on his side and closer to his back. He could just make out the redness spreading just under his ribs. Yeah, there was definitely a stinger stuck in him. He felt for it with careful fingers.

"I see it." She hesitantly pushed away from the door.

He hiked his shirt a little higher, twisting slightly into the light in an attempt to find it in the mirror. Instead what he saw was the librarian duck in up to his side a half second before her fingers brushed his waist.

"Got it." She washed it down the sink and then retreated to her spot by the door.

"Thanks," he said, forcing a smile. The place where she'd brushed him tingled a little, but he told himself it was the bee venom. "All right, so... what exactly is it that we're supposed to talk about?"

"Oh, um... no. No, it's okay. I-I've changed my mind."

"About?" he pressed.

She hugged her waist with one arm, clapping her hand to her forehead while she laughed in an unsuccessful effort to dispel the awkwardness. "I can't believe I'm doing this."

"Doing what?" he coaxed, not quite sure if he was growing impatient with her or curious.

Her laughter died. "I really wish she'd asked you about this first; it would have made it so much easier."

Once upon a time, back before he became a felon, he'd thought he could read women pretty well. Lord knows, he knew physical attraction when he saw it, and back before Grams pulled that stunt with anaphylactic shock and the bee sting, this little woman had definitely been looking at him through the eyes of someone who was physically attracted. She didn't know his history, though. And once she did, that physical attraction was going to die the kind of death only a guy who had absolutely nothing to offer a date could die.

"Talk about what?" he asked.

"Your grandmother," she said, chewing at her bottom lip.

"What about her?"

"She..." A slow flush of pink rose to stain her cheeks, and she almost winced as she said, "She said you could stay at my place... for a while."

Kurt stared at her and he was proud of himself, really. He didn't say a single one of the curse words currently running through his head.

Monday really had ceased to be subtle about it, and now so too had his Grams.

She hadn't just set him up. She'd set him up on a booty call.

Chapter Four

It sounded bad even to her own ears, but Scotti was so rattled she couldn't think of another way to say it. "She said you can stay at my place for a while."

He blinked, his face completely devoid of any discernable expression. "I beg your pardon. She said what?"

"But now I'm having second thoughts," she stammered, heat burning a slow flush up into her cheeks because of how he kept staring at her. "I really don't want you to get hurt."

He was so good-looking, so built. When she'd touched his side, his skin had been soft, and warm, and muscularly hard just underneath the velvety-smooth surface of him. He even smelled good, like old spice and coffee and, oddly, French fries.

She loved French fries.

He arched his eyebrow. "*You* don't want *me* to get hurt?" He stared at her with no expression on his face and arms as thick as small tree trunks, folded across his chest. It felt like forever before he shook himself out of his thoughts and said, "I don't know what the both of you have plotted out, but I don't think I want any part of it."

It was weird, and she didn't understand why, but when he stepped toward her, for the smallest half-second, she felt like she was trapped in this room with Gopher. Her flinch was immediate, and he stopped coming when she flattened herself against the door, her hands flying up to stay him from coming any closer.

He stopped. She still couldn't read his expression, not when he looked at her hands, and still not when his gaze rose back up to lock on hers again.

He wasn't being threatening. She didn't have any reason to be scared of him. She offered another shaky laugh, trying her very best not to be scared.

"I'm sorry." She patted the air, still scrambling to figure out which would be the bigger mistake: hiring this man to protect her, or not hiring him.

"For what?" he asked, even more cautious than before.

"Because I'm explaining this so badly. Look," she blew out a calming breath and tried again. "I would like to proposition y—" she caught herself, shook her head and changed her mind, "N-not proposition, per se. I mean, I want to hire you." She looked at him hopefully. "For your services," she expanded her explanation when he only stared, both eyebrows arching high.

"All right." Clearing his throat, he unfolded his arms long enough to take hold of her shoulders. His tone softened, "I don't want you to take this at all personally, because you seem like a very nice lady. But I don't think I'm interested."

Desperation mixed with the knots in her stomach, twisting at her insides until she felt sick from the pressure. "I can pay you. I can. I-I took everything I could out of my savings. I wouldn't expect you to do it for free," she protested on his behalf, her desperation only sharpening its teeth when he shook his head. "Your time and skills are worth compensating, I understand that!"

"What the hell has my grandmother been telling you?" he blurted, then quickly held up a silencing hand. "No. Scratch that. I don't want to know. It doesn't matter anyway; the answer is still no."

"Please, I don't know who else to turn to."

"As beautiful as you are?" She recoiled, stung when he actually laughed at her. "I highly doubt that."

She flattened herself against the door. "I am begging you!" Sadie hadn't said he would be this hard to convince. If only she'd known, she'd have been better prepared. She'd have grabbed her phone from her purse so she could show him the pictures. She'd have brought her copies of the police reports. She'd have got down on her—Scotti dropped to the floor, clasping her hands in pleading. "Please," she tried again. "You don't understand how desperate I am!"

"Try doing two years." Bending, he caught her about the

waist and physically picked her all the way up off the floor.

With a startled squeak, she grabbed onto his shoulders as he swung her around and set her down again, this time on the other side of the sink. Out of his way.

"It's not that I don't appreciate how you're feeling," he said. "God knows, I've felt this way many times myself. The important thing is not to act on those feelings, particularly not with perfect strangers whom you've only just met."

"We may not have met before, but I do know all about you," Scotti said quickly. "Sadie's been telling me about you for years. I know you've been away, working for the state. I know your favorite TV show is *M*A*S*H*. You like your fried chicken extra crispy and smothered in gravy along with your mashed potatoes. You're a connoisseur of vanilla ice cream. You've got a scar on your hip from an accident you were in when you were a teenager. You went to school with Robbie Knievel's cousin's son, and you've got a Jones for *Phantom of the Opera*. You've even got the soundtrack in four different languages."

"You forgot married," he said, as if that should matter.

Scotti flapped her arms in the smallest, most hopeless of shrugs. She was a little disappointed, but not terribly surprised. He was a handsome, sexy-looking man. Of course, he'd be married. "That's okay. I don't mind."

Instead of placated, he actually got annoyed. "My wife might!"

"I don't see why she should. I said I'd pay you."

"That's even worse!" he snapped. "Look, I'm flattered. Really, I am. But there's just no way in—" He bit off an exasperated sigh, looked up at the ceiling, and then grudgingly back at her. "Look, it's not you; it's me."

She listened, trying hard to understand.

Her confusion must have been obvious, because he said, "I should be so much further along than where I am right now in my life. I'm not set up right now for complications. Now, you're pretty, okay." He waved an arm out toward the closed bathroom door. "You've obviously got Gram's vote, and annoyed as I am with her right now, that does count for something. But I am old school, okay? I like to get to know the people I do this with. I like to take them out, maybe catch a nice dinner, get to know them and develop feelings—"

She swallowed hard. "I didn't realize that was part of the service."

"I'd also like to get to a point where it's not called a service," he added. "I'm not a bull in a pasture."

"I didn't mean to offend you. I just didn't realize." She blinked rapidly, but her disappointment was overwhelming. She didn't know if he was her last chance or not, but it felt that way. She honestly didn't know where else to turn. "Would it make any difference if I promised to do anything you say? I mean, *anything*. I know things are bound to get rough, and I'm sorry about that. But I really will try to do whatever it takes so you don't get hurt. Won't you please reconsider?"

He came down to her level so fast, she jumped back. But like with the door, the bathroom only had so much space. She bumped up hard against the sink, and the next thing she knew, she was pinned to it, trapped between his arms as he gripped the edge of the sink in both hands.

"All right now, little girl," he growled, and her stomach both seized and sizzled, and all at once, every knot inside her suddenly relaxed. They only relaxed just a little, but it was the most relief she'd had in months. "When it comes to rough rodeos, you would not be my first ride. That's number one. Number two, what the hell kind of librarian are you?"

"I-I—" she stammered, the knots doing tumbling acrobatics all over again. She didn't know if it was because every breath she took right now was scented with the spice of his deodorant, aftershave or a combination of both, or if it was because of his very nearness. He was a big man. A veritable mountain of a human being, with great big hands that were right now gripping the sink behind her, and that look on his face brought her inner Little snapping to the forefront. It was completely inappropriate to let her out right now.

"No," he said, cutting her off. "You might think Gram has told you everything you need to know, but I guarantee there are sides of me even she didn't know and which would send you running if you did. Maybe I've been away too long, but asking a total stranger to have sex with you is a little more than just desperate. It's dangerous. And rough sex?" He shook his head with an incredulous laugh. "Lady, you're lucky we're not in the kind of relationship where we're having sex, because if we were, that would cost you. It would cost you big."

Scotti froze mid-breath, her eyes widening. She didn't realize her jaw had dropped until she had to pick it up enough to gasp, "I'm sorry, what?"

He stopped now too. One startled minute bled silently into two, before he shifted how he was leaning, although he didn't back away. He remained looming over her, still smelling so good, still seeming so threatening. Scotti tried not to, but her nipples were tingling and her bottom was prickling, every inch of it consumed in this crazy crawling sensation that gradually moved down between her legs until, no matter how hard she tried to tighten her thighs, the tingling took root, filling her pussy with a warm flush of need.

He cleared his throat. "What?" he parroted back at her, the realization that they'd been talking about different things becoming embarrassingly clear to both of them.

"You think I was asking you to..." Her cheeks scalded hot, and then even hotter still as she realized what that also meant. "Y-you think I need t-to pay... you..."

She couldn't even finish that.

"Something tells me I've just sunk this Monday to new record-setting lows," he said.

She had no idea what he meant by that. She was still trying to wrap her mind around... "Women pay you for that? You're *that* good?"

Now, it was his turn to blush, but before he could say anything, she shook herself and threw up her hands.

"I mean, no! That isn't what I meant at all! Hell no, even! Good heavens!" She looked down at the prison of his arms and his chest, and then her gaze dipped lower, and her eyes widened when she saw the notable tent bulging at the front of his jeans. "Oh..." She spun to face the mirror and, because that didn't help at all, quickly locked her eyes on the ceiling. "You, um... you should, I don't know... put a little cold water on that."

She saw it in the mirror when he looked down at himself. He jumped back from both her and the sink, as far as the little bathroom would allow him. Her stomach tingled. Her nipples did too. She wasn't sure who she was more embarrassed for: him for misunderstanding her intentions, herself for having explained what she wanted that badly in the first place, maybe herself again for being so far below his type standards that he had to say no this emphatically, and lastly, for both of them because now it was all just so... awkward.

"Sorry," he said, adjusting his pants.

"No, no," she soothed, her voice a little squeaky and too high-pitched. "It's good."

His Daddy bits were really kind of sizeable.

Scotti closed her eyes, willing herself not to think about it. Too late. Not only was the image burned into her brain, but her tummy had gone all melty, and she wasn't at all sure she knew how to pull herself together so she could look at him without blushing.

Clearing his throat twice, Kurt cupped his lean hips in his big hands. He regarded the floor long enough to collect himself. Then, raising his eyes to look at her in the mirror, he said, "I'd like to start over, if possible."

Her tummy did flipflops just at the sound of his voice. She pushed on it with both hands, willing the gymnastics to stop. "Okay."

"My name is Kurt Doyle."

He said he liked rough sex, her brain recalled, and her face flushed several degrees hotter.

He said he liked rough sex and that doing that with him would cost me big.

"Hi, Kurt," she said weakly, still staring at the ceiling, willing her face to cool down and her heart to stop pounding the way it was. "I'm Scotti Moore."

"Hello, Scotti."

Tingles ran through her just at the sound of her name on his lips.

I'll bet he spanks.

He cleared his throat. She stole a peek at him, but nope—there was still bulging in the front of his pants. She snapped her eyes back to the ceiling.

I'll bet he puts on black leather and goes to the dungeon parties where he ties up the girls and flogs them unmercifully.

Oh, God. She was going to start giggling any second. Not because that mental image was funny in any way, but because it hit way too close to home and her nerves just couldn't handle it.

I'll bet they call him Daddy when he does it, her Little self said.

That right there all but killed her nervous giggles. She hadn't had a Daddy in a long time. Not a real Daddy, anyway. Not since Gopher.

"Now that I'm done embarrassing us both with assumptions," Kurt said, clearing his throat. "How about you tell me what it is you really want to hire me for?" He held up his hand before she could do more than open her mouth. "I'm not saying I'll do it. As it happens, I did get hired for... something this morning, so..."

"It doesn't hurt just to hear me out, though, right?" she said hopefully. Just thinking about Gopher helped kill her embarrassment, as well as her amusement. She even forgot she wasn't supposed to look at him. She turned around, needing to see him directly instead of just his reflection.

"Sure." He shrugged, then propped himself against the wall, making himself comfortable to do just that.

"I... I need help." Funny, it didn't get any easier to say the second time around, either. The police hadn't believed her. The dispatchers at 911 didn't believe her. What if he didn't believe her, either? What was she going to do then?

Except there was nothing on his face that said he was doing anything but listening, mind and ears both wide open.

"In what way?" he asked.

Clutching her hands tight together, she braced herself for rejection. "I want to hire you to be my, um... my bodyguard."

He cocked his head, and his gaze swept over her once. "Why on earth do you need a bodyguard?" He immediately caught himself. "That came out wrong. I didn't mean to say it like that. You have a perfectly nice—"

"No, no." She fluttered her hands, trying not to be stung by that. "It's fine."

"Normally, I'm a little more polite and a lot more charming than this. Just not on Mondays." He rubbed his mouth sheepishly. "Why does a librarian need a bodyguard?"

Scotti hesitated, chewing at her bottom lip. "I've got a problem," she hedged. "My Da—I mean, my..." She hesitated. Her what? She'd managed to stop herself before calling him her Daddy-dom. Ex-boyfriend hardly seemed appropriate, but what did that leave? "M-my ex," she stammered, cringing a little, but that would just have to do. "He's doing things—"

"You don't need me. Get a restraining order."

"I have. He's not the sort of ex who pays attention to that sort of thing."

"Then call the police."

"I did." She wrung her fingers, bracing herself even harder. "They don't believe me. Nobody believes me." That he only looked at her, quiet and waiting, gave her the strength to say, "He broke in last night. I called 911, but they said I could go to jail for trying to prank them and not to call back."

Almost imperceptibly, his eyes narrowed. "Do you think you're in danger?"

She wrung her hands so hard it hurt. "I think he's going to cut me up, stuff me into a million Ziploc baggies and stow me in the freezer next to the Christmas ham, and he's going to do it while I'm on the phone, begging someone to come help me."

She stopped. Not because she'd said everything she could, but because her chest had tightened too much to let her continue. She nodded instead, and prayed he took her seriously.

He blinked. A slow tic of muscle leapt along his jawline, bulge and release, bulge and release. "What exactly do you want me to do?"

"Well," again she bit her bottom lip, hesitating. "Most of his visits come at night. You know, he walks around the house, treads all over my flowerbeds, tries the windows and doors... and no matter what I do, he gets in. He always gets in."

Clench and bulge. There went that tic of muscle again.

"I-I was thinking, maybe two things. First, if he sees that I'm no longer alone, then maybe he'll stop coming by. They say abusers don't like to out themselves as abusers. They'll stop if they get caught. So, if you're there to see what he does, then he won't want to do anything, right? He'll just go away. Right?"

He had no reaction. "And two?"

"If that doesn't work, then maybe we can catch him,

hopefully before he does me any serious harm, then one of us could call the police, and they could lock him up. At least long enough for me to move safely to someplace else." He wasn't saying no. He wasn't laughing at her, either, and that emboldened her. "Like I said, I'm willing to pay you. Not much, but would three hundred a week be all right with you?" When he only looked at her, she cleared her throat. "It's all I can afford. Three hundred a week. For about six weeks. All right, not about. That's it, in a nutshell. Six weeks."

"Miss…"

"Scotti."

"Scotti," he said. "I am not a bodyguard. You need to know that right up front. I used to be a police officer, but I'm not *allowed* to be that anymore. I've never guarded a person. Except for what I've seen in the movies, I don't even know what that job entails. I agree you've got a problem, but I would seriously recommend that you find someone with real experience in the kind of protection you need."

"I can't pay enough to interest anyone else," she confessed, her heart sinking. He was saying no. Whether or not he believed her didn't matter. He was still saying no. "Please don't feel pressured into doing this. It's just that I've got this feeling like I'm running out of time."

Kurt took a deep breath. "Look, it's not that I want to see you get hurt, but I don't think my grandmother has been totally forthcoming with everything you need to know about me."

She didn't know why he would be worried about that, but she moved close enough to lay her hand on his shoulder and did her best to lay those fears to rest. "You'd be surprised, I think. She's really very proud of you. She talks about you all the time."

That ticcing muscle leapt as he clenched his jaw. "Did she happen to mention that I've been at the Two Rivers Correctional Facility for the last couple years?"

Scotti nodded. "She said you had a job with the state. Were you a guard? Talk about a tough job, herding all those dangerous convicts. You probably know how to handle all sorts of situations. She's the one who said you'd be perfect for this, and I have to say, I kind of agree."

"I worked in the laundry, actually."

She opened her mouth, not at all concerned with what his actual job had been, but then stopped as she realized what that meant.

He smiled, arching both eyebrows again with exaggerated humor.

"Oh," she said, a tiny thump of shock hitting her. "You mean you were an inmate."

"I was, and don't worry"—he shoved off the wall—"I won't hold you to your proposal."

"Oh, but don't you see? That's even better! You don't know my ex. You don't know just how bad Gopher can be."

"You dated a man named Gopher?"

Dated was such a mild word for it; she winced. "It doesn't matter, really. What does matter, is that I'm going to need someone who's strong and tough. Indomitable. A man's man. Burly and rough." She was starting to feel desperate and trying hard not to let him hear it in her tone. "Someone who can think with a crafty and—and criminal mind!"

"Thanks," he drawled, but that twist at the corner of his mouth said he might not be taking it as the compliment that she'd meant it to be. "You don't even know what I did to get put in prison."

"I'm not concerned." She tried to laugh as she said it, because frankly, she was trying not to think about that. Sadie had only ever said he'd been gone because he was 'working for the state.' He seemed very nice. Nothing about how he looked or spoke to her suggested he was a bad person. On the other hand, people didn't get put in jail for no reason. Ever the optimist, she tried to find the silver lining. "You were only in the pokey for a short time, right? Whatever you did, it couldn't have been that bad of a crime."

"Pokey?" he echoed. He seemed about to correct her, but stopped himself. He stared at her for a long time, his jaw clenching, bunching and releasing until finally, he shook his head as if shaking himself from his thoughts. "Fine. You know what, it doesn't matter. It's better than bussing tables at Pirate Pete's with a paper squid hat on my head. I'll do it, but you're going to listen to me. I say jump, you say how high, got it?"

"Oh, absolutely!" she crossed her heart with her fingers.

"And, I'm not killing him for you. I'm going to make that clear right up front. I'll help you get moved to a place where Ferret—"

"Gopher."

"—whatever, can't find you. I'll even put you in contact with someone at the station who won't brush you off. After that, it's up to you and the police to sort out a more permanent solution to your problem. Right?"

Like Frosty the Snowman under the heat of the sun, all her fears melted inside her. "He's going to leave me alone after this, isn't he?"

Kurt didn't answer, per se. What he said instead, was, "I'm going to take Grams home now, but then I'll come back. Now, can we please get out of the men's room?"

Grinning, Scotti led the way.

Chapter Five

The sun was on his shoulders, along with Grams's book bag. The ninety-two-year-old woman was shuffling along beside him, smiling and humming to herself. The wily old con artist.

"You need to stop telling people I was a cop," he finally said, as they walked home together.

"I didn't tell anyone you were a cop," she countered.

Touché. True, he was the one who'd revealed that and judging from Scotti's reaction, he didn't for a second doubt that had been a slightly shocking reveal for her.

"All right," he decided. "Maybe what I ought to say is, you know I'm not a cop anymore. So, what's the play here?"

"No play."

Bullshit.

"I know you better than that."

"Can't a woman be concerned about a friend in trouble?"

"Grams," he warned.

The old woman abruptly stopped walking and turned on him. "Now you listen here," she sternly began.

"Grams..." he warned again, facing her now too. He frowned. Cars were whizzing by on the road. Someone honked, but whether it was because of them, he wasn't sure. It might have been. If it was, he knew it couldn't look good. He was a big man, facing down an elderly woman, and he was the only one watching this who knew what a manipulative force of nature this 'old woman' could be.

"Don't you 'Grams' me," she replied. "You haven't always been here, and yes, that's not your fault. But I've made a friend in that young lady. She's sweet, she's kind—"

"She's got good childbearing hips?" he pointedly asked.

"You noticed that too," his grandmother teased, lightly

smacking his arm with the backs of her fingers. Chuckling, she started walking again.

Tsking, nowhere near as amused as she was, he fell into step beside her again. "This is not going to go the way you want it to."

"And how," his grandmother asked, "do I want this to go, exactly?"

"I'm not going to date this woman." He was firm on that. His life wasn't set up for dating.

"She's pretty, though."

"It doesn't have anything to do with pretty."

"She used to be just your type."

"You have no idea what my type—"

"Submissive," his grandmother said with relish.

He stopped walking. "Okay, now we agreed we weren't going to talk about that."

"A grandmother never forgets when she walks in on her beloved—"

He barked a laugh.

"—grandson," she said, covering her heart and staring up at him with exaggerated innocence, "spanking the hell out of some chubby little blonde with a pink stripe in her hair and a 'Daddy's Whore' tramp stamp right across her—"

He stopped again, his turn now to round on her. He pointed at her. "Stop. I didn't ask her to get that tramp stamp."

It was his most authoritative finger and his most authoritative tone. Back before he went to prison, when he was attending the occasional dungeon party or when he had a Little girl to soothe the Daddy-Dom need inside him, that combination of voice and finger were usually enough to shut all misbehavior down. Unfortunately, his grandmother was immune to both, and he had no recourse. No matter how much she needed it, he wasn't about to spank her.

"It didn't displease you."

No, it certainly had not. But he wasn't going to talk to her about that anymore than he was going to spank her. "I also didn't ask you to come home from Bingo early."

"Oh," the old woman huffed, flinging off his complaint with a flap of both hands. "You've been spanking your sweethearts since you were six and playing house in the backyard. You were always a Daddy. Man up!" She lightly smacked his chest with her hand. "Be a Daddy now. Protect that girl, no one else has been." Once more walking down the sidewalk toward the apartment he'd shared with her since he'd been released from prison, she flapped her hands again and called back over her shoulder, "She needs you!"

It had been a long time since he'd had a Little, the Daddy-Dom inside him whispered.

He was absolutely not going to take the 'Little' his grandmother found and brought home for him, like a little lost puppy.

Stifling a sigh, he followed her. "I took the job."

"Of course, you did," she said smugly. "I raised you right. Plus, you were never able to resist helping when you knew someone needed it."

God, he hated being predictable.

"Straighten up," he said, because he literally had nothing else to tease her about. "There's nothing wrong with your back, and you know it."

Chuckling, the old woman cast him a wink. "People are always watching, honey. Always leave them guessing."

"Con artist," he said, not unfondly.

"Convict," she replied in kind, then giggled. "Did you hear how that just rolls off the tongue? Oh, I like that much better than 'cop.' Convict," she enunciated, and giggled again.

God help him.

* * * * *

"So," Scotti asked, feigning cheerfulness while he knelt on her porch under the amber glow of her too-dim porch light and tried to pick her lock. "Why do you hate Mondays?"

"Because of crap like this." Snatching a quick glance up and down the dark, residential street behind them, Kurt returned his attention to the task at hand. He jiggled the bobby pin in the front door lock. "I can't believe I let you talk me into this."

"They don't send you to jail for breaking into your own

house. Besides, I do have a key. I was just so rattled when I left this morning, I think I left it on the entertainment center. On any other day, I'd show you this trick I have with the kitchen window, but that's how Gopher got in last night, so I put a wedge in it after he left." She bent, hands on knees as she watched him jiggle the hairpin. "Something tells me breaking and entering was not your criminal career of choice."

He stopped fidgeting with the door long enough to give her a dirty look. "Do you want to do this?"

"No," she said, contrite. "I'm not trying to be a pain. Also, you don't have to yell at me."

"I'm not yelling," he growled, once more back to the task at hand. "I can't yell. I don't have any voice left after you slammed my hand in the car door."

"That was an accident." She sounded hurt. "I was nervous and never saw your hand. I've already apologized three times for that. You need to forgive me and move on."

He flashed her another quelling (he hoped) look just as a sharp metallic click emanated from the lock. "We're in."

"Oh," Scotti said as he opened the door. "Awesome."

Only she didn't sound like it was awesome at all. She flashed an immediate smile when he glanced at her, but it never once touched her eyes. She gripped her hands, folding them tightly over her stomach as he swung the door wider, and made no effort to step inside. She was scared to go in, he realized. Honestly, legitimately scared in a way that someone 'pranking' 911 or staging things to get attention from friends, family, or even police wouldn't be.

Admittedly, he'd only been halfway convinced of her story back at the library when he reluctantly accepted the job. He became completely convinced when he stepped inside, flicked the main light switch on, and suddenly a carpet-muted thump hit the second-floor ceiling almost directly above them.

He immediately flicked the light back off again.

Her breath turned instantly shaky as they both looked up at the popcorn ceiling.

"You said you lived alone," Kurt softly clarified.

She nodded every bit as shakily as her breathing had become.

"No dogs or cats?"

She shook her head, her hands betraying all the fear that her face was trying so hard to hide.

"Stay here," he told her. "Don't move from this spot unless someone other than me comes down these stairs. If someone does, I want you to run like hell for the nearest neighbor, understand?"

Wringing her hands, she nodded.

As quietly as he could, Kurt crept across the tiled foyer toward the carpeted stairs leading up. It was surprising how fast that old 'cop' feeling returned. He could almost feel the weight of his utility belt, the coolness of the flashlight he no longer carried in one hand and the textured grip of the gun at his hip in the other. This wasn't an emergency call, though, he reminded himself. And he no longer had a badge on his chest. He had to remember that.

He was just stepping up on the first stair when suddenly the light above him flicked back on again. He snapped around to find Scotti, not on the spot he'd placed her on, but just inside the door, her hand still on the light switch and her wide eyes locked on the ceiling.

Bounding back to her, he slapped the light back off again, grabbed the front of her librarian's blouse and shoved her back out onto the porch. "What are you trying to do?" he demanded in a whisper. "Get me killed?"

"Don't you need to see where you're going?" she stammered.

"All that light is going to do is illuminate a nice open target—me—so your ex can start shooting!"

"Yes, but then you can see him too, and you can shoot back," she argued, sounding both small and frightened. She was trembling and clinging to herself.

She's just your type, Grams had said.

And God, right now in the dim glow and shadowed darkness on her porch, staring down into those fear-filled eyes, he could see it. It was the helplessness. He'd always been drawn to small, scared, and helpless.

Kurt shook himself. This was not the time or the place, not when there was a potential intruder upstairs.

"I," he told her very slowly and clearly, "do not have a gun. That would be a violation of my parole. I would get put back in prison." He pointed at her. "Stay put," he repeated. "Stay quiet, and let me do my job."

For the second time, he left her there in the doorway and quietly approached the stairs. Halfway up, he heard another sound. It was soft, just a whisper of a footstep on carpet, but when he cautiously turned the stairwell corner and peeked above the top landing, he saw nothing. Nothing but a hallway, with three open, shadowy doorways and a Disney princess nightlight splashing the colorful heroines of its movie *Frozen* up on the ceiling and walls. He waited, listening, but whoever might be up here with him was quietly listening back.

Climbing the last few stairs, his back to the wall, he approached the first open doorway. Without looking inside, he closed it. If the intruder up here was in that room, then they were now blinded to his movements and would have to come out in order to commit to their next intention. They wouldn't be able to do it quietly; the opening of this door would be his warning. He'd worry about that when and if it happened. For now, he'd closed off one potential avenue of attack. There were two left.

The next open doorway was a few feet down and across the hall from him. It looked like a bathroom. The gaping shadow-filled archway at the very end of the hall offered a little more detail. The faint paleness suggested lamplight from the street below, filtering in through a window. He could just barely make out the shadow and shape of a bed beyond the cover of the partially ajar door.

He switched walls, putting that one to his back as he moved up to the edge of the bathroom threshold. He closed that door, too. There was only one potential avenue of attack left open to him.

As he slipped past the bathroom, something caught his eye. Directly across from him, the wall appeared to be creased. Thinking it first a trick of the shadow and nightlight, he reached out far enough to touch it, letting a stroke of his fingers tell him what his cop's brain had suspiciously determined already. Someone had carved a line in the sheetrock three-fourths of the way down the length of the hallway, from the first door he'd closed, all the way to the bedroom at the end.

Scotti's bedroom? He moved a little closer to the open door. The shadows on the bed were moving. A whisper of a cool night breeze brushed his face. He peered around the threshold just far enough to see the fluttering curtains of her bedroom window, moving in the darkness, showing the escape the intruder had taken when whoever he was—Kurt was fairly certain he could solve that mystery in one guess—had heard them unlock the front door.

The bed looked weird.

Lumpy. The only un-neat thing he'd so far seen in Scotti's house. Admittedly, he hadn't seen much of it. Just the foyer downstairs, a glimpse into the bathroom, in which he'd noted the orderly counters and towels tidily hung up, and then this room. Where there was nothing on the floor. Her dresser drawers were closed, with nothing on top but a hairbrush and what looked like a handful of Lego superheroes having a choreographed battle. She had a second dresser, long and low, plus an overstuffed rocking chair in the corner by the window, both of which were buried under a small mountain of stuffed animals.

The mountains were neat, though. The Legos were neat. The dressers were neat.

The bed was lumpy.

The intruder was gone, so Kurt turned on the light.

The bed had been stabbed and slashed, the pillows destroyed, the blanket and sheets shredded.

"Gopher, my friend." Kurt didn't realize he was going to say anything out loud until he heard himself growl, "You've just fucked up."

* * * * *

Someone was definitely in the house with them. Hovering on the porch where she'd been left, for one perfectly terrifying moment, Scotti couldn't think what to do. Should she stay here? Should she go inside just in case Kurt needed her? Her heart was beating so hard and fast. She pressed her sweaty palms flat against her thighs. This was it. The moment of confrontation with her ex, which she had been dreading ever since she told him she didn't think it was working and he told her, "Well, isn't that just too damn bad?"

That had been almost a year ago, and, here she was, standing on her front porch like a petrified rabbit caught in the headlights of an oncoming car.

Dredging up a slim slice of courage, she took her first hesitant step into her own house. Then she took another. She kept her eyes trained on the stairwell, but all she kept thinking was how neither she nor Kurt had anything with which to protect themselves if this went bad. Gopher was getting braver.

She wasn't. She definitely wasn't.

One of them really ought to be armed, and if Kurt couldn't do it, then that only left her.

Her home didn't have a fireplace, so there were no iron pokers, and she was too scared to go as far as the kitchen. The garage was even further, but the bathroom was right by the bottom of the stairs. Gathering the shreds of her courage, she grabbed the only thing she could think of—an aerosol can from under the sink. Without any lights to see by, she didn't know what she had. Probably sink cleaner. By the time she was back out and at the base of the stairs, her nerves were jittery. To the point that when she heard an ominous creak from the hallway above, she almost dropped her can.

She braced herself. With the coolness of the can tucked up in her palm, one finger on the trigger, she got ready. *What* she was ready for, she wasn't quite sure. She liked to think she might be brave enough to charge upstairs in defense of her bodyguard, should he yell out, but she felt every bit as likely to scream and run away.

There it was again. Another footstep, another creak approaching the top of the staircase.

Kurt wouldn't be coming back unless he knew there was no one upstairs; if there was no one upstairs, he wouldn't be sneaking. It was Gopher, her brain supplied. It had to be.

Swallowing past the lump in her throat, she raised the aerosol spray. Her hand was shaking, but she didn't back down. She'd done a lot of backing down these last few months, but she wasn't alone anymore. It wasn't like before. Someone believed her now.

The footsteps picked up, starting down the first flight of stairs. There was only the minute space of the landing and the corner between herself and her tormenter now. Cold panic tickled through her.

Oh God... Oh God...

A huge shadowy shape lurched around the hallway corner, and Scotti waylaid her intruder with a scream of warbling hysteria. It was only after she'd completely emptied her aerosol can directly into his face, did she realize that shadow was much too big to ever have been Gopher.

The manly bellow that followed wasn't Gopher's, either.

"Agh!" Kurt yelled, tripping on the stairs as he vaulted backwards. He fell, spitting and swiping at his eyes, shouting, "What the hell is wrong with you, woman!"

Running to the light switch at the bottom of the stairs, she quickly flicked it on. Sure enough, Kurt was on the ground, grinding the heels of his palms into his eyes and swearing.

"Oh, Kurt, I'm so sorry!"

A loud thump hit the small, decorative roof on the east side of the house, over the study window and underneath her bedroom, and crashed into the bushes on that side of the house. When brush rustled near the door, she panicked all over again.

Running to the door, she slammed and locked it without ever catching sight of Gopher. Kurt was still wheezing and rocking on the stairs when she reluctantly came back to the stairs. She winced as he coughed, scrubbing at his red eyes.

"What the hell did you use on me?" he demanded.

Looking down at the label in her hand, Scotti sheepishly told him, "Feminine hygiene spray. Hypo-Allergenic. With aloe."

She supposed she ought to be glad it wasn't sink cleaner. She could have blinded him.

Peeling open red-rimmed eyes, he glared at her.

"Floral, um... fresh?" Scotti said, though she knew that wouldn't make a difference. Biting her bottom lip, she guiltily tucked the spray can behind her back.

He got up off the floor, looking mad as hell. It made her

flinch when he pointed at her with a very big, very angry finger. "That's one," he growled and stalked past her into the bathroom to wash his face.

Feeling awful, Scotti stood on the stairs where he left her. One what, she wondered as she watched him go, but she kept the question behind locked teeth. Maybe later, when he'd had a chance to calm down, and if nothing else happened to keep him this upset, then maybe she'd dredge up enough courage to ask.

Chapter Six

"Where are you going?" Kurt called from the kitchen where he was installing fresh, functioning locks on all the windows.

"I'll be just a minute," she called back, halfway up the stairs and heading toward her bedroom. Once there, she closed the door as softly as she knew how, collected Bat Bear from amongst her friends on the dresser, and then put herself in the closet. She didn't turn on the light. There was no way to keep Bat Bear from knowing what was happening, but she didn't need to see it. Nobody needed to see it. That was why she crawled all the way into the back corner of her closet to sit cross-legged behind the shielding skirt of two long winter coats, several full-length dresses and her old graduation gown. Hugging Bat Bear to her chest, she buried her face into the popcorn-smelling back of her head, and did her best to cry in a way no one who wasn't supposed to know would hear.

She just needed a minute, she told herself. Then she'd go back downstairs and pretend that dealing with this didn't scare her or bother her at all. Just one, short, tiny minute.

She never got it.

With her face buried against her stuffie, she never saw the cracks around the closet door light up, but there was no missing the boom of Kurt's low voice snapping out, "Answer me right now, where are you?"

Scotti yelped, she startled so bad. She clapped her hand over her mouth, but the damage was already done. In the next instant, the closet door swung open and there was Kurt. Hiding behind her dresses, she couldn't see him, but she knew he'd have no problem seeing her. Or, at least, the cross of her legs and half of Bat Bear being strangled in her arms.

Hangers scraped on the bar overhead and the coats and dresses parted, spilling her in light. Kurt looked at her.

Great, now she wasn't just sad, she felt stupid too.

"It's not what you think," she said, sniffling and swiping her eyes dry on her wrist.

Lowering himself to squat in the closet doorway, he folded his hands between his knees. He really was a big man. He practically radiated calm and patience. Like even when he was picking her front door lock and patience had been the last thing he'd been feeling. She couldn't read his expression now, but at least he wasn't yelling at her. Nor was he laughing.

"I didn't want you to see the bed yet," he finally said.

Oh. She tsked, touched by that kind of sweetness, especially coming from someone she'd sprayed in the face with feminine hygiene product. "Oh, that." She waved that aside with her hand. "Don't worry about that."

"You already knew," he guessed.

"Yeah, I was, um... under it at the time." She rolled her eyes in an attempt to help them stop watering. "It's okay. I'll duct tape it in a minute."

He looked from her, to the bed, and then back to her again. With all the expression of a marble statue, he stood up and held out his hand.

Insides tightening, she reluctantly passed Bat Bear over, but he didn't take it away from her. Instead, he took hold of her wrist and pulled her up out of her closet and to her feet. She didn't know he was going to hug her until his arm came up around her, steering her into his chest before she could slip past him and leave.

His strong arms wrapped her the same way she did Bat Bear, and she was completely unprepared to withstand it. Hugs like this were rare for her. She'd only ever had it one time before, and that was with Gopher, back when he first asked if she'd like him to be her Daddy-Dom. After several munches with her local dungeon group (the first that she'd managed to work up courage enough to attend), followed by a handful of private 'dates' over coffee in a public coffeeshop, she'd been just starry-eyed enough to say yes. He'd said everything right. He'd been gentle, and kind, and they seemed to match on so many levels. But look how that had ended—she'd had the best Daddy in the world... for the first few months; she'd had the Daddy from hell ever since.

But, even when he was Hell Daddy, sometimes Gopher would hug her.

It had been a long time since any of his hugs had felt like this. Kurt was bigger than Gopher. His arms were burlier, and they hugged her as if his embrace were all that were holding her together.

Maybe it was, because without any ready defenses to throw up between them, she could tell herself all she wanted that there was nothing in this hug. That bodyguards hugged their charges all the time. That Kurt was just being kind, and sympathetic, and friendly, but her inner Little still triggered. And triggered hard.

She clung to Bat Bear just so she wouldn't grab Kurt and cling to him instead.

When he asked, "Are you okay," into the top of her hair, she nodded immediately, but she wasn't. That she had lied could not have been more apparent when, within seconds of it, she then burst into tears and ugly cried all over his shirt.

She wouldn't have blamed him for being uncomfortable, but if he was, he never showed it. He simply tightened his arms and held her close until the worst of the storm was over. Then with his hand on the back of her neck, he steered her out of her bedroom to the bathroom down the hall. Standing in front of the mirror with her bear still hugged in her arms, he wet a washcloth in cool water and quietly bathed the heat of her tears away. Her eyes felt raw, but the pass of the cloth eased both the heat and the hurt, and helped her feel a little more like normal by the time he was done.

A sad normal, but then sad was better than scared, and she'd been living in 'scared normal' for quite a while.

"Look at me," Kurt said, rinsing the cloth one last time, wringing it out and hanging it up on the hand towel ring by the sink.

Scotti looked at his reflection in the mirror.

"Try again." Hands on his hips now, he waited until she dutifully turned around and looked up at him directly. "Repeat after me: I'm safe now."

She felt beyond ridiculous repeating such a thing. She wasn't safe. Not now, maybe not ever again. After tonight, she could see Gopher hanging back long enough for what little money she had to pay Kurt to run out, and then Kurt would leave and she'd be right back to where she'd started. Only then it would get worse.

He might actually, possibly even kill her. And she had absolutely no way to stop him.

When she stayed silent, Kurt raised a warning eyebrow and in low warning tone, said again, "I'm safe now."

"I'm safe now," she echoed. Her stomach was so full of knots that had been trip-rope tight for so long now that she'd stopped feeling it. Until, in spite of herself, they relaxed. It was just a little bit, but the relief was overwhelming. Tears burning at her all over again, she stared locked on his eyes, soaking in all the reassurance she knew better than to ask for.

"Say, I live under new rules now," Kurt commanded, softly, his tone as strong as sturdy iron girders.

"I live under new rules now." The knots relaxed even more; pure relief flowed through her. She almost closed her eyes under that wave of raw, heartfelt release, but he stopped her.

"Look at me."

He was her lifeline, and she knew the way she was staring at him must have reflected that to a pathetic degree. And yet he didn't seem at all uncomfortable by that. He wasn't retreating in the slightest. Instead, he advanced half a step, bending slightly over her and with nerve-shivering authority said, "Nothing of my life before today matters anymore…"

She repeated him.

"None of those rules and restrictions still matter…"

She said that too.

"Because my new Daddy says so," Kurt said in stern emphasis, as if he knew but didn't even care that those words shivered her all the way to her soul.

"B-because my new Daddy says so," she whispered, every knot in her stomach tightening strangle tight in an instant before slowly melting away.

"And my new Daddy," Kurt told her firmly, "will keep. Me. Safe."

She swallowed hard. Her mouth felt weird, like it was someone else's as she parroted that back to him.

"Now, here are the rules." He counted them off on his fingers. Like all the rest of him, even his fingers were huge. "Rule number one: You go nowhere without my knowledge and permission, is that understood?"

She nodded.

Arching both eyebrows, he waited, one finger still ticked.

Fidgeting with the seams of Bat Bear's costume, she hesitantly said, "Yes, I understand?"

His eyebrows arched higher. She'd never had someone look at her with half this much severity, at least not without her panicking. "Yes, what?" he calmly demanded.

Her heart fell into her stomach. Her already shallow, strangling breaths quickened, growing even more shallow. "Yes, Daddy," she whispered.

"Rule number two" —he added another finger— "all of your incoming house phone and cellphone privileges have been revoked. When either of your phones ring, I am the only one allowed to answer. You may make all the outgoing phone calls you like, so long as you aren't placing phone calls to the rodent. From this day forward, if I find out you've called that man, there will be serious consequences. Do you understand?"

"Yes, Daddy." Her knees buckled slightly. Her legs actually felt shaky and weak. She wanted to sit down right here on the floor at his feet.

"Are you safe at work?"

She nodded.

"Rule number three. I will take you to and from work. From the moment I leave until I return again, you will stay inside the building where there are witnesses who can protect you. If you leave for any reason without my knowledge and permission, there will be serious consequences. Do you understand?"

She was going to cry again. All of a sudden, it was like being back in the men's room at the library and he'd just accepted the job of being her bodyguard. She was so happy, her voice quavered. "Yes, Daddy."

"Rule number four. You do what I say when I say it. I do not tolerate arguing for argument's sake, defiance or disobedience."

She had to swipe her eyes dry again. It was hard to talk, so she nodded. "O-okay."

"Break any of my rules in any way, and there will be consequences."

She nodded, hiccupping and sniffling.

"Take a bath," he told her. "I'll be back in a minute."

He stalked out of the bathroom, stopping abruptly in the hallway when she followed him out. She almost ran into him, but jumped back half a step when he turned on her with a frown.

"What did I just tell you?"

"Take a bath?" she stammered, wide-eyed.

"What's rule number four?" He held up the appropriate number of reminding fingers.

Scotti retreated another step, more stunned than scared. "I-I—"

"You do what I saw when I say it."

"B-but..." She pointed through the bathroom in the direction of her bedroom. "I need clean clothes..."

He went from holding up his hand to catching hold of the back of her neck. "Turn around."

He didn't wait for compliance, but physically turned her until she was staring back at her own wide-eyed expression.

"Hands on the sink," he told her.

This wasn't happening. Holding Bat Bear by the arm, she braced herself against the edge of the counter. With the heat of one broad hand clamped on the back of her neck, she stared in growing disbelief as she watched his other arm swing back. It was all so surreal. Right up until the flat of his other hand came cracking down hard across the center of her skirt-clad backside. She was still in her professional librarian business attire. That business attire did absolutely nothing to soften the force with which he spanked her.

He only swatted her once.

It startled the hell out of her, and stung like a fury.

Her mouth rounded in both shock and admiration. Her new Daddy had a really hard, spanking hand.

When he let go of the back of her neck and physically turned her around to face him again, he had her full and complete attention. "Did I tell you to go get your clothes?"

"No, Daddy." *Don't rub your bottom*, she told herself fiercely. *Don't rub*, but already her hands were back behind her, cupping her butt with Bat Bear's solicitous help.

"What did I tell you to do?" he reminded.

"Take a bath."

"Are you going to keep arguing with me?"

"No, Daddy."

"Then what should you be doing right now?"

She immediately kicked off her comfortable flats and dove for the tub to insert the plug and turn the water on.

He watched, hands on his hips once more. "What's your bear's name?"

"Bat Bear," she said, whipping off her dress belt and then her bracelet, and then floundering because those were all the safe things she had to remove. After that, some part of her was getting intimately uncovered with her new Daddy standing right there, watching her.

"Put Bat Bear on the counter," he said. "She doesn't need a bath right now, and you don't want to ruin her."

Right. Rattled as she was, she just wasn't thinking. She slipped past him to put Bat Bear down, and when she turned, he'd already walked out of the room. He'd even closed the door to the barest of cracks, giving her privacy. Feeling almost as weirdly titillated as she was unnerved, she shucked out of her clothes in record time and hopped into the bath, yanking the plastic fish-tank curtain so it stretched from wall to tiled wall. She sat down with the hot water still running and hugged her knees to her chest.

A few minutes later, he returned long enough to lay a clean towel, clean underwear and her pink bunny footie pajamas with 'It's Night Night Time' in bright purple and silver glitter across the butt. She had half a dozen perfectly grownup nightshirts folded in her dresser, right next to where those pajamas had been.

They were her Littlest pajamas. They even had a butt flap.

Easy to take down. Easy to spank her through without taking the whole thing off.

She couldn't handle this. Lying back in the tub, Scotti sank into bathwater that came up to her ears.

Holy shit. She had a new Daddy.

How the hell had that happened, again?

Chapter Seven

Kurt taped her mattress, stuffed as much of her pillow as he could find into her pillowcase, and then found another pillowcase on a shelf in the closet and shoved the first pillow into it. He wasn't Martha Stewart, but he made her bed and vacuumed the floor while he waited for Scotti to get out of the bath. Then he checked all the windows, tested each lock to make sure they were sound and put 'buy new locks' on his mental checklist for tomorrow. It would take some time, but he was going to completely change every lock before the weekend.

Then he would change her phone numbers.

Then he was going to start work on a restraining order, and he was going to make a few old friends who might not hold hostile feelings toward him aware of what was going on.

Before he was done here, he would get someone to listen.

And once she was as safe as he could make her, then and only then would he figure out a way to extricate himself from the problem he'd just made.

What. The. Hell.

God, everything that had just happened upstairs in the bathroom had just happened so damned *naturally*. It was the bear, it had to be. When he'd heard her walk upstairs, he'd chased after her. He'd wanted to prepare her. The last thing he wanted was for her to see what had been done to her wall and her bed and panic.

I was under it at the time, she'd said, hiding in the back of her closet, just like any Little he'd ever known might do. With tears still running down her face and that blatantly *I'm so sad* expression on her face, just like the last Little he'd been a Daddy to would occasionally have, especially when coming out of punishment time. And that bear cuddled to her chest… oh, that bear had been the clencher.

She's a Little ran through his head like a skipping record. The entire time she sat gazing up at him from her hiding place in the closet, to the entire time they'd been in the bathroom— him counting out a new list of rules that would irrevocably redefine the rest of their relationship together; her, with those big, wide eyes locked on him and that teddy bear in the Bat Girl costume still clutched in her hand and her hands on her bottom as she tried not to rub, and occasionally failed.

He made up a bed for himself on the floor at the foot of hers, with his head positioned so he could see at a glance both the window and down the hallway.

Those looks of hers were going to be his downfall. He was very susceptible to Little looks. They brought out the protector in him, and damn Grams for the wily old woman she was, she knew that too.

Jesus, had Grams seen that look on Scotti before? Did she know Scotti was a Little? Did she know about the time he'd spent in his old BDSM group, back before he went to jail and back before he had a felony strike against him that would make it difficult for him to get back into a reputable dungeon from now until the day he died? Responsible dungeons ran checks on their members. Some only banned people with sex offenses. His old dungeon banned felonies period, and Kurt knew he had made that unforgiving list before he'd even gone to trial.

His friends there had turned their backs on him without even giving him a chance to explain. Dana had made sure of that.

He could never go back there.

He could never go back anywhere.

If he had Scotti, he wouldn't have to, the devil on his shoulder whispered.

Like he'd ever just settle for a relationship with anyone for no reason other than because it was easy.

Like Scotti was easy, his devil scoffed.

He tuned that voice out and cranked up the stubborn in his soul. The only relationship he was going to have with Scotti would be the employer/employee relationship. He was her bodyguard, that was it. He was here to protect her to the best of his abilities, not to get attached.

Like he had anything to offer anyone, anyway, the devil whispered.

Exactly, he agreed.

Keep it simple. Keep it professional.

Don't fall under the spell of those big-eyed Little looks.

"Can I get out of my bath now?" Scotti asked from the doorway, startling him.

On his knees fussing with blankets, he froze when he saw her—hair wet from being washed, her face clean of makeup, dressed in her pink bunny footie pajamas and Bat Bear dangling from its arm at her side.

Oh Jesus.

He was so screwed.

"Are you hungry?" Somehow, he managed not to sound like he was strangling on the rising tidal wave of need crashing down on top of him.

She nodded.

"I'll make you a sandwich." He stood up, but a part of him wanted more to open his arms and see if she'd rush to throw herself against him, flinging her arms around him, burying her face into the crook of his neck and making herself small in that special way that brought the big, bad Daddy-wolf in him snarling to the surface.

She needs protecting like few you've ever known. Funny, how his inner angel sounded just like Grams.

You're not a cop anymore, the devil replied. His protection powers were severely limited these days.

His sandwich-making powers, however, were topnotch. He led the way to the kitchen with her following like a duckling at his heels.

She had a nice, modern kitchen, with a cooking island that did double duty as a table. On his side, there was a stove and a shiny array of copper pots and pans on a hanging rack above it. The fridge was at his back, the double sinks to his left, and more than enough cupboard space to make searching for whatever he needed an extensive game of hide-n-seek until he figured out the layout. On her side, she had a row of four barstools, and she promptly parked herself on one.

"I could make *you* a sandwich," she offered, as he began hunting down the bread. "On top of the fridge."

"It's fine," he said, pulling it down. "It's all part of the service."

Her fridge was every bit as neat as the rest of her house. Things were organized—fruit in the fruit bin, vegetables in the crisper. A thin drawer below had sliced deli turkey and a wide assortment of cheeses. He dug past the Havarti and Provolone until he found Swiss. Pulling a bag of red grapes and baby carrots from their bins, and a squeeze bottle of mayonnaise from the door, he shut the fridge and came back to the island.

"One sandwich or two?" he asked, pulling out enough bread for three.

"One," she said.

He added another pair of slices and put the bread away. "Crusts on or off?"

"Off," she stammered slightly. "I do eat them, though. I like to pretend they're French fries."

He cocked an eyebrow, tried not to smile lest she think he was doing it at her expense, and made up four turkey and Swiss sandwiches, crusts off on one.

He began a search of the cupboards again.

"Top set," she said. "Two to the left of the sink."

He found the plates and made their suppers: a sandwich and a short stack of crust 'fries,' along with a handful of baby carrots and some grapes for her; three sandwiches, the rest of the small bag of baby carrots and a sprig of grapes for him.

"What did you go to prison for?" she asked, setting Bat Bear up beside her plate so the two of them could share it.

"No stuffies on the table," he said between bites, and she stopped what she was doing and moved Bat Bear to sit on the stool beside her. She glanced at him to make sure that was all right; he allowed it. "I was stupid. I thought I could trust someone, and I couldn't."

"Your partner?" she said.

"You watch too many movies." Polishing off the first sandwich and picking up another, he said, "Does the rodent know?"

She didn't try to play stupid and pretend she didn't know

what he was referring to. He liked that about her. He also liked how she hunched her shoulders and suddenly found anything and everything in the area so much more interesting to look at than he was.

"Yes," she admitted.

"Tell me you did not let Chipmunk be your Daddy."

"Gopher," she corrected. "In my defense, he introduced himself as Robert."

"When did he become the Groundhog?"

A corner of her mouth twitched. "Our third date, I think. And the way he said it made it sound more like a job than a name. You know, like go-fer. He'd go-fer this, or go-fer that."

"We have those in prison too," he said, unimpressed. "They're nowhere near as nice as Morgan Freeman makes them out to be."

"Morgan Freeman?" She blinked at him.

"You never saw *The Shawshank Redemption*?"

"No." Finishing her 'fries,' she started on her grapes.

"Carrots too," he said automatically.

"I only like them when they're candied or cooked with ham. You know, so they taste good."

"Carrots, too," he said again, and making a slight face, she ate one next. "The movie doesn't matter. What does matter, is that you knew Mouse-boy was a rodent and you still agreed to date him."

"He was still being nice back then."

"Uh huh." He watched her pick up a carrot, then pick up her sandwich. Taking a bite of sandwich, she tried to palm the carrot. "Not if you know what's good for you."

The corner of her mouth grimaced, but she put it back on her plate. She looked at him. "I really don't like them."

"You've only got four more to go."

She made herself eat another one, and he made a mental note of her anti-preference.

"Where did you meet him?"

She voluntarily stuffed the last three carrots in her mouth and stared at her plate while she chewed, probably so she wouldn't have to answer him.

"That's okay. I can wait." He ate a grape.

Her face turned a slow, hot shade of red. Halfway done with her carrots, she tried to add a bite of sandwich.

"When Daddy asks a question, he expects an answer," Kurt warned.

She blushed even brighter, but reluctantly put the sandwich down and swallowed what was left in her mouth. "D-do you know what a munch is?"

"Yes, I do." He didn't at all like that answer, and he especially didn't like the mental image it came with. He could easily see her walking into one of those dungeon meal-meetings, where old and seasoned members met with newbies for the sole purpose of inviting them to play. Often newbies were called what they were: fresh-meat. Scotti in her business-casual librarian's clothes and Bat Bear dangling from her hand by its arm... that was mouthwatering fresh-meat, right there. Put a pair of pigtails in her hair, and he could easily picture all kinds of Doms vying one another to be the first to break her in.

And the Dom who won had been a fucking Gopher.

"You're not going back there," he said, finishing the rest of his grapes. "In fact, you and I are going to have a sit-down regarding dungeon safety rules, and until that happens, you're not going to go back to any meeting, munch, or dungeon-oriented coffee get-together, I don't care how public it is. Not until I am confident that you can keep yourself safe."

Like he had a right to make such a sweeping decree on what she did with her life.

She called him on it, too. "Now, wait a minute—" she said, sitting up a little straighter on her stool.

"No," he cut her off. Not because he had the right, but because all he had in his head now was the mental image of her standing in front of a bunch of salivating Daddy-wolves. Only now her librarian's outfit was that of a schoolgirl, with her long blonde hair done up in ribbons and pigtails, and Bat Bear still dangling at her side as she twiddled her fingers and shyly introduced herself, saying, "Hi, I'm Fresh-meat."

Hell, no.

"Oh, hell, fucking no," he said, hotly. "You continued to date a man even after you found out his name was Squirrel—"

"Gopher."

"I am making a point," he told her. "And that point is, your decision-making process—if you even have one, considering you made him your Daddy—is suspect. If I find out you've gone back before we've had that talk, I don't care if I'm your bodyguard then or not, I will bust your butt so hard, you won't sit for a week. A month. A month of damn Sundays, do you understand me?"

She frowned. She also squirmed on her stool, that single swat he'd given her in the bathroom no doubt giving her an inkling of what he'd just threatened her with.

"If I'd known you were going to be this bossy, I'd have found another bodyguard," she grumbled.

"No one else would take the job," he reminded. "You're stuck with the bossy, hard-up convict who busts ass. If you think for a second, I've got any problem busting yours again tonight, I seriously suggest you think again."

She cast the frown she meant for him at her plate. He let her keep her mutinous thoughts to herself, and they finished the rest of their supper in absolute silence.

Chapter Eight

It was the strangest and yet the most comforting thing in the world to be lying in her bed with a brand-new Daddy she'd only just met stretched on a pallet of blankets on the floor near her feet. Her bedroom door was wide open. She could see the bright colors of her Disney princess nightlight splashed up on the walls and ceiling of the hallway. That was comforting. But there was also this big ol' yawning darkness down by the stairs leading out into the rest of the house, and the last time she'd been lying here, staring down that hallway, Gopher had been walking up it with his knife in his hand.

Lying on her side, Scotti drew her knees to her chest. She picked at the edge of the duct tape holding her blanket together. After asking whether she had the money for it, Kurt had told her tomorrow they would stop at the store to buy a replacement. Honestly, though, she wasn't in a hurry. She really liked this blanket. It was soft and warm, even in winter, and the perfect blend of stark black and pale pink blossoms, just like the blossoms on an ornamental Chinese cherry tree. She liked pink. Pink was her favorite. She liked flowers too. Pick after nervous pick, she shredded the edge of the duct tape.

Quiet though she thought she was being, with a heavy sigh, Kurt said, "Do you want your Bat Bear?"

"No stuffies in bed," she said automatically. "Beds are for other things."

She could have bit her tongue, but the damage was already done. Already Kurt was sitting up far enough to look at her over the foot of her bed. The dim light of the nightlight had no problem illuminating his irritation.

"Is that the Gerbil's rule?"

She worried the edge of the fast-shredding duct tape,

although not for the same reason as before. "Yes."

"Who's the Daddy in this house right now?"

"You are," she said, soft as a whisper. Soft or not, her stomach did crazy acrobatics when she said it. Complete with a flush of warm heat that lit up her insides and flowed, like a river of warm, slow chocolate, down into parts of her that wouldn't at all have minded being eaten. Her thighs tensed, and then tensed again when Kurt got up off the floor. He didn't need any extra light to locate Bat Bear from amongst the other stuffies she had stacked up on her dresser. When he held it out to her, she took it and hugged it to her chest.

"In this house, stuffies are allowed in bed," he said.

God, he was good.

Scotti closed her eyes when he pulled the edge of the blanket up to her chin, tucking her and Bat Bear in together. She thought she felt him touch her hair, but when she opened her eyes, he was only looking at her and he was doing that marble statue thing with his face again. After a moment, he went back to his blanket and laid down.

The floor could not have been very comfortable. Her bed was a queen-sized, so it wasn't as if they couldn't share it. The river of chocolate grew just a little more molten and flowed just a little faster. Slow thumps of pressure were building up between her thighs, no matter how tightly she squeezed them.

Hugging Bat Bear, she said, "Do you want to sleep up—"

"No," he said.

No, of course not. That wouldn't have been very professional, for either of them. And as bad as that low needy throb she kept feeling was now, she couldn't imagine how much worse it might become once all she could feel was the weight and size of him stretched out on the mattress beside her.

Now she really couldn't sleep.

Picking at Bat Bear now instead of her blanket, Scotti asked, "Is there someone out there missing you because you're sleeping here?"

"Grams has late-night TV to keep her company," he said. "She'll be fine."

"No, I mean someone like me."

"I already told you, I've never done this before. You're

my only client. Go to sleep, Scotti."

"No," she persisted. "I mean, do you have someone... like me."

"People who just get out of prison don't get the luxury of having somebody," he said. "They get to get their lives back together first." His tone dropped into those low notes of warning that she was starting to recognize as preceding a threat to her sitting abilities. "Close your eyes and go to sleep."

She closed her eyes, but her mind wouldn't quiet, and so they only drifted open again a few seconds later. "You did have someone, though, right?" she asked, and even though he sighed again, added, "Someone like me? Once upon a time?"

"Scotti..."

"But you're too good a Daddy not to have had somebody!" she protested.

She could practically feel the waves of disapproval rolling off him and that frustrated her. She was just asking a question. That he wouldn't answer and satisfy this one niggling curiosity was killing her! He'd jumped on the Daddy train without her saying one word; there had to be a past Little out there who, once upon a pre-prison time, had looked up to this aggravating lout and felt safe because she was his.

Or maybe the Little was a boy?

"Was your Little a guy?" she asked. "Is that why you don't want to talk about it? I'm not a mean person. I promise I don't kink shame or judge."

He sat up again. "Do you need a hot butt?" he asked, evenly.

"No, but—"

"Two," he said sternly.

That stopped her. Her tummy and her butt both tightened sharply at the threat, but that minute tightening didn't last beyond the knee-jerk shock of hearing it. "You can't start at two," she grumbled. "It's illegal to start at two. What happened to one?"

"One was on the stairs earlier tonight when you sprayed me in the face with that female crap."

"But that was hours ago! You can't just pick up where you left off, you have to start over every time!"

Kicking back his blankets, he got up off the floor.

"How high do you count?" she asked in increasing nervousness as he came back around to her side of the bed.

"Nowhere near high enough to help you now," he said, stripping the blanket back off her.

"No!" She all but threw Bat Bear in her haste to get away, but he caught the back of her neck before she could do more than roll onto her tummy. "No!" She scrambled to get her hands and knees up under her.

He killed her flight instantly when he said, "Fight me and I'll use my belt."

An ominous tingle broke across the entire surface of her bottom. Oh. Oh yeah, he had definitely been someone's Daddy at some point in time.

"W-wait," she stammered, but he didn't wait. He pulled the Velcro tabs apart and dropped the seat on her pajamas, exposing the very thin cover of her underwear and a bottom already cringing.

"Wait, please!" she cried, her already high voice rising in panic when he hooked the elastic waist of her panties and took them down as far as he was able. The butt flap wasn't a large opening, but it was large enough. He bared her bottom to the tops of her thighs.

"Daddy!" she bawled, but already he was bringing his open hand down in that first mighty swat and he didn't seem to care at all that she burst into tears almost before he started.

"I do not wait," he said over the top of her cries and the thunderclap smacks of his flat palm raining down one hard swat after the other. "When I tell you to do something, you do it. When I start counting, you stop what you're doing and pay attention, or this is what you'll get."

He gave her no warmup and no pause between spanks to help her deal with the pain before the next swat fell. He simply paddled her, hard and fast, covering every inch of her bottom in sharp, staccato slaps that stung like a vengeful fury. And then hurt. And then really, really hurt. A lot.

It was the kind of hurt that quickly became impossible to hold still for. It didn't matter that fighting back would mean the belt. With each new bite of pain he smacked into her, her body instinctively took on a life all its own. Her feet came up off the mattress. Her legs scissored, her hips twisting and bucking, desperately seeking out some way in which to move that might tuck her bottom safely out of his punishing hand's reach. But no matter how she moved, she couldn't escape; and no matter how piteously she cried, he didn't stop. Not until the whole of her butt was wounded, throbbing, positively on fire with unbelievable hurt, every bit of which had been delivered with nothing more lethal than his bare hand.

"You're not supposed to spank that hard," she sobbed.

Pulling her panties back up over her aching bottom, he covered her with the Velcro flaps and then the blanket. He picked up Bat Bear, which had fallen on the floor sometime during the struggles, and handed it back to her. And then, with his hands braced on the mattress beside her, he said, "Are you going to go to sleep now, or do I need to spank you some more. Because I can do this all night if I have to, but I guarantee you're going to like the next one you get from me even less than this last one."

It took everything she had not to grab her bottom in both hands and rub the fire out. He wasn't holding her hands. She could have grabbed onto anything she wanted to, but naughty girls weren't allowed to rub. They didn't get to ease the pain. They were only allowed to endure.

Bending, he pressed a gentle kiss on the top of her head. "Daddy doesn't give gentle or fun spankings for bad behavior."

When he went back to his bed and lie back down, she very discretely let go of her bear long enough to touch her pajama-clad bottom under the covers. She didn't rub. She'd just gotten spanked and while, technically, no rubbing wasn't a rule he'd laid down, she didn't want to be caught misbehaving again. Not tonight, anyway.

She didn't rub. She just held, feeling the burn that radiated through all the layers of her clothes and into her marveling hands.

Oh, he was definitely somebody's Daddy before this.

And now he was hers.

She ought to do something nice for him, so he'd know she wasn't just naughty, or whiny, or needy. So he'd know she appreciated what he was trying to do for her. Not just the spanking, but everything. From sandwiches to crusty fries, to sleeping at the foot of her bed so she would feel safe.

Tomorrow, she decided. Tomorrow she would find a way to do something nice for him.

With any luck, her bottom will have stopped hurting by then.

Chapter Nine

It was bright and early on a nice, solid, sensible Tuesday. Kurt was standing at the cutting board in the kitchen, dressed in only a towel when Scotti's cellphone rang. He knew, because it was sitting on the counter right next to his phone, and he was in the middle of tearing open a brand-new package of pre-sliced cheese when the screen lit up in big, block letters that spelled out 'Gopher.'

And so it began.

Picking up the phone, he hit the button. "The number you are trying to reach is currently busy or hates you," he said, by way of hello. "One would have thought you'd have realized that last night when you were diving headfirst out the window into the bushes."

"Go away or else," a man's voice growled cryptically back.

In the middle of making two ham and cheese sandwiches for breakfast and four more for lunch, Kurt wedged the receiver between his shoulder and ear and went back to spreading mayonnaise over a half a loaf's worth of bread. "Or else, what?"

"I'm not playing with you. I mean it, go away."

"I don't take threats from vermin."

"You'll take them from me. Or else."

He licked a dollop of mayonnaise off his thumb. "Is that the worst the all-mighty Ferret can come up with?"

"Gopher."

"Don't care. Not leaving." Suddenly, his phone lit up now too and vibrated, buzzing against the counter. Picking it up, Kurt looked at the unfamiliar phone number.

From Scotti's phone, Gopher's voice dropped ominously. "I can make you go."

"I'd love to see you try, Guinea."

"Guinea?"

"Pig."

"Bastard." Gopher hung up the phone.

Switching phones, Kurt answered his. "Hello?"

"May I speak to Kurtis Doyle, please?" a man's voice replied. For some reason, the voice sounded familiar, though at first Kurt couldn't place it.

"Speaking," he said cautiously.

"Mr. Doyle, I'm not sure if you remember me, my name is—"

Recognition hit like a sickening twist that went straight through his gut to his groin. "Emerson Davis," he said along with the man on the other end of the phone. The district attorney who had called him a dirty cop and sent him to prison for two years, costing him everything, including his career, and all for something he hadn't done. "What the fuck do you want?"

"I realize I'm not the person you probably want to hear from right now, but last night I received a visit from a young lady named Krissy Degrassi—"

"Now you listen to me," Kurt interrupted, the twists in his gut erupting into temper so hot and volatile that for a moment all he wanted to do was slam his phone into the bottom of the sink. "Running into that girl yesterday was sheer fucking misfortune. I wasn't following or stalking her, if that's what she told you. I was applying for a god-damn job."

"You're not in any kind of trouble," the DA calmly assured.

"Then I don't have to tell you shit," Kurt replied, and hung up the phone. He promptly blocked the number, because the way his temper felt right now, if Davis called back, he really would throw his phone and he simply could not afford a new one.

Setting his cell down instead of dropping or throwing it was a massive personal achievement. One he'd be proud of later, once he was done being pissed.

Hands braced against the counter, he closed his eyes and simply breathed. In... then out... until shaking his head, he let it go. He had more important things to do than dwell on Dana, Krissy, or the DA who had sided with her to ruin his life.

Swallowing past his anger, he shoved back off the counter and made himself finish what he was doing. His hands only shook a little as he piled a thick variety of turkey, chicken and baloney over half the bread, a stack of cheese and tomato slices over the other half, and mashed both sides together in a therapeutic show of emotion six times. Stuffing four away for later, he was much calmer when it came time to make breakfast and lunch for Scotti. Her sandwiches were peanut butter with strawberry jam. He cut the crusts off both, stuffed one set of 'fries' in a Ziploc baggy along with one sandwich, then took the other into the living room on a small plate. He set it on the dining table and, after adjusting his towel, sat down across from where Scotti was folding a basket of freshly dried laundry.

"So," he said conversationally, taking a huge bite. "How's the underwear coming?"

Her hands stopped folding. Her head still bowed and moving only her eyes, she looked at him. She bit her bottom lip.

Kurt sighed. "Let's see them."

Reluctantly, Scotti dug into the unfolded pile and slowly withdrew a pair of his undershorts, still stained bright pink from when she, in a moment of helpfulness, kidnaped his clothes while he was in the shower. He knew exactly what had done it, too. His red and white-striped cabin boy's shirt was now red and pink-striped. His tights were pink, too. He could already hear the sensitive pirate and I-wanna-sing-and-dance jokes now.

In other words, his Tuesday had become Monday Part Two.

"I can't get the color out of your tights and shirt either," she admitted. She offered the smallest wince of a smile. "You know, a lot of guys wear pink these days."

He just chewed his food. Mondays and Tuesdays, now there were two days of the week gunning for his personal destruction. To be brutally honest, he wasn't holding his breath for a happy Wednesday either. He frowned at his pink shorts in her hands until she self-consciously tucked them back out of sight beneath the unfolded laundry pile.

"When do you have to be to work today?" he finally asked.

"Eight to noon on Tuesdays. When do you work?"

"Two to eight," he said, unenthused. "Just not on the fry machine." He could see his pink-striped shirt peeking out between the plastic mesh of the laundry basket. "Maybe they'll have another uniform my size," he said, although he didn't have much hope. Things like that didn't happen on Mondays, and he suspected the same would hold true for Monday Part Two.

"How are we going to do this?"

"We're going to handle this by me accompanying you to your work where I can keep my eye on you, and then you are going to accompany me to my work, where I" —he sighed heavily— "am going to be the only thirty-two-year-old pirate on the payroll in pink tights, shirt and shorts. And, where I can also keep my eye on you. You might want to bring something to do."

"I don't know," she said, looking at the laundry. "That doesn't tend to turn out well for me."

"I can handle pink underwear long enough to earn a paycheck and buy some more."

Her shoulders slumped. "Pink underwear, Gopher. I make a mess out of everything I touch."

She looked genuinely unhappy, too. Not unhappy as some Littles did when they wanted hugs or cuddles, and so picked at themselves because they didn't know how else to get it. Kurt was very familiar with that kind of behavior. Krissy's mother had been one of those, and before he went to prison, he used to cuddle the hell out of her whenever she got like this. He'd cuddled her even when he knew it was an act meant to manipulate a compliment or forgiveness out of him for some slight misbehavior.

That 'act' had been like a default setting for her. Hell, she'd even done it the one time she'd come to visit him after he'd been sent to prison. Because of Krissy.

"Please don't ask me to take you out of here by putting my baby in," she'd said, with those giant crocodile tears building in her eyes. And god help him, but if it hadn't been for that thick pane of glass separating them, he'd have reached through and tried to comfort her still.

Standing here in Scotti's house, looking at her as she

looked dejectedly at her basket of semi-pink clothes, most of which should have been white, Kurt would have sworn there were worlds of difference between Dana and Scotti. But, he also knew he couldn't trust himself to see this clearly. The Daddy half of him was a cuddler and a forgiver. Always had been; always would be.

"It's just clothes," he told her. "Two months from now, no one is going to care that a red got in with the whites and the color ran. The ghosts of Gopher might linger longer, but I'm going to get rid of him and two years from now, if you can even remember his name, you're going to shake your head and wonder at whatever decisions led you to making him part of your life. But that's life," Kurt said. "Nobody goes through it perfectly or without mistakes. Which means, you don't get to beat yourself up for the mistakes you do make."

She looked up at him, shoulders hunched. "That's easy for you to say. You don't have a Gopher in your life."

He snorted, shaking his head. "No, I do not."

When she bowed her head back to her laundry, he blew out another sigh, shook his head at himself again, and came back to the table to sit down beside her. He set his last sandwich on the table. Taking the laundry away from her, he set it on the floor and physically turned her chair around so she had no choice but to look straight at him.

"No," he told her again, "I do not have a Gopher." Smothering another sigh, hardly able to believe he was doing this, he grudgingly confessed, "I have a Dana."

She blinked. "Who?"

"I dated her for about four years. She was my girlfriend and my Little. I met her at a party, not unlike the one you say you met your Gopher at. We became play partners at the dungeon we both attended. Then we became more than that, and eventually we moved in together. Her daughter, Krissy, was the reason I went to prison. She was a... troubled girl. She never really warmed up to me, but I didn't know how badly she hated having me in her mother's life until one day at work, they were running training exercises for the K9s in the parking lot and one hit on my car. Where Krissy got the drugs, I have no idea, but she planted enough to get me convicted for felony possession with intent to distribute. Both she and her mother testified against me in open court, and I lost everything. My badge, my life... my Little, everything. I also did two years in general population with a lot of angry convicts, every one of whom knew I was a cop."

"That's awful," Scotti softly said. As genuinely sad as she had been only a moment before, she now looked every bit that sympathetic. "I'm so sorry."

Kurt shrugged. "Mistakes were made."

"Yeah," she agreed, "but not by you. That never should have happened."

"And what Rodent is doing to you should?" he countered.

"No," she scoffed, a corner of her mouth twisting, but her brow furrowing as if in confusion. "But that's different."

"How?" he challenged. "Why? Because you're a submissive, so you ought to just take it?"

She rubbed her hands and her eyebrows drew even closer together, but she didn't argue.

"That's the kind of argument battered women use to defend their abusers. Tell me you're not doing that." Slowly, deliberately, he took hold of the arms of her chair and pulled her close, parting his legs to draw her as near as their two chairs would allow. Her knees brushed the inside of his thighs, but he only stopped pulling when he ran out of space between them. Even more slowly, much more deliberately, he leaned toward her. Close enough to smell the subtle coconut scent of her shampoo and the linen fresh scent of the dryer cloth residue on her hands. "Do you know what I think you deserve to take?" he asked her, his voice dropping low in spite of himself, and every rapid-firing synapse in his brain screaming for him to stop.

To get back.

To put as much distance in between him and this woman as he possibly could before it became—

She raised her eyes to his, womanly reluctance at war with Little innocence in the depths of baby blue eyes so alluring that a man could fall face-first into the pool of her and happily drown.

—too late.

"What?" she whispered.

"Kisses," he replied, every inch of him an idiot because he couldn't seem to make himself stop.

She tried to smile, but it was breathy, a shaky echo of the kind of smiles she'd flashed him last night when for a few short seconds at a time she'd been comfortable enough in his presence to forget she was supposed to be scared.

It was like being trapped in the library men's room all over again.

Or standing in her bathroom upstairs like they had been last night, with his hand still stinging from the swat he'd landed on her skirt-clad backside and her attention raptly fixed on his reflection in the mirror.

She was tripping every single one of his Daddy triggers, and she didn't even seem to know she was doing it.

In the kitchen where he'd left it, the phone rang, but Kurt made no move to answer it and after only a few shrill cries, it went quiet again. He didn't care. He was much more intently focused on the way Scotti was rolling her lips together, as if savoring the touch of his mouth upon it.

When her gaze dipped to his lips, even knowing he shouldn't, he said, "A woman like you, Scotti, should be made to take kiss after kiss, after toe-curling kiss. Until your whole body can't bear to take another one."

She shivered.

Were her nipples perked? Were they beaded up against the inside of her shirt, pushing stiffly out against the cloth, reaching toward him in the hopes they might receive a chance touch of his hand?

Don't look, he told himself. He was torturing himself with a woman he barely knew.

Oh, the devil on his shoulder cooed, *but it's worse than that, isn't it? You're not just torturing you; you're torturing her too.*

Somewhere in the bowels of the house, he heard the hard buzz of a dryer go off. Almost at the same time, in the kitchen his phone started ringing again.

"I better get that," he said, shoving his chair back.

Bursting into awkward laughter that came out just a little too shrill to be normal, she jumped up too. "Yeah, I, uh... I should get that too."

She grabbed her laundry hamper and all but ran with it downstairs. She only looked back at him one time, but when she did her eyes were huge and hurt and perplexed all at the same time.

What the fuck was he doing?

Pissed at himself, Kurt stalked back to the kitchen. Half expecting the call to be from District Attorney Dickface on a different phone line, he was ready to block that too. But no, it wasn't an unknown number this time. It was Grams.

"What's up?" he said, answering on the fifth ring.

"Are you going back to jail?" Grams asked bluntly, without her usual cheery greeting. In fact, she sounded tense and far more serious than he was used to hearing from her.

"No, why would you—"

"Why is a DA calling my house, and why does he want to talk to you?"

Stifling a curse under his breath, Kurt threw an exasperated frown to the ceiling first, and then the floor. He rubbed his eyes. "I ran into Krissy yesterday. He probably wants to tell me the restraining order is still in effect."

"Which only brings us right back to my original question," his grandmother insisted. "Are you going back to jail?"

"No," he said firmly. "I didn't do anything wrong."

"Like that stopped them from putting you in prison the first time," she said, rare notes of bitterness creeping into her voice. "What are you going to do?"

As if there was anything he *could* do.

"I'm going to get on with my life," he told her. "I'm allowed to have a job. If Krissy doesn't want to see me, she can frequent another fast food squid house. I don't care, but I'm not running from her. And I'm sure as hell not running from DA Dickface."

"You're still calling him that?" Grams asked, with a chuckle that made her almost sound back to her normal self.

"He doesn't deserve to be called anything else," Kurt said. "And if he thinks for one second a phone call from him is going to make me panic and run, then he doesn't know me any better now than he did the first time he locked me up."

Only the guilty ran. Kurt wasn't guilty, and he didn't run. Not from anybody.

Chapter Ten

"Is that him?" Doris O'Conner asked, rising up on tiptoes to her full height of four feet and nine inches. She peeked over the checkout counter at where Kurt was unobtrusively sitting on the floor below Scotti's desk, reading a book on World War II Japanese submarines. She adjusted her bifocals and squinted to get a better look.

"That's him," Scotti replied, doing her best to sound cheerful and not at all self-conscious that she had a man sitting practically under her desk at work. She wasn't an idiot. A hell of a lot of pornos started this way, and everyone in the library knew he was here. He'd gotten up and down several times—to go to the bathroom, to get another book to read, to get a drink of water from the water fountain in the hall. If everyone in the library knew he was here, then maybe someone (i.e.: Gopher) outside would know it too. So, apart from keeping her distracted and embarrassed and flustered all day long, how was this helping again?

"What a hunk," Doris mooned.

"The hunk can hear you," Kurt drawled, not looking up from his book.

"What a hunk," Doris repeated, this time in a whisper. "If I were thirty years younger, I might give you a run for your money over a guy like that." The old woman smiled, wrinkling her nose, and gave Scotti's hand a friendly slap. "Have you gone to bed with him yet?"

"Uh," she flushed, her whole body—her face especially—radiating with embarrassment. She shot Kurt a look, but if he'd heard that, he didn't react. He only turned the page of his book. "No, Doris. It's not that kind of friendship."

"Why not? You're a woman; he's a man. What more do

you need? Besides, Sadie says he's hung like a—"

"Doris!" Scotti whisper-shouted, cutting the old woman off but not before her wrinkled hands measured out exactly how 'hung' he was.

"She's his grandmother," Doris protested. "She ought to know. She's also telling everyone, so if I were you, I'd get a move on before some young hussy sneaks in from the sidelines and grabs him right out from under our noses. I saw Miranda giving him the once over while you were at the card catalog. Just because she's got big breasts doesn't mean she's the better woman, honey, but that man has been in jail for two years, so you'd better get crackin' on that whoopie before she lures him away."

Mouth agape, Scotti quickly checked to make sure that Kurt wasn't listening. "How did you know he was in jail?"

"What do you think 'working for the state' means?"

"Landscaping?" she shot back, then forced herself to lower her voice all over again. "Construction... building... I don't know, but—" Her mouth snapped shut as her mind suddenly focused in on the rest of what Doris had said. She leaned across the checkout counter, coming down to the old woman's much shorter level. "Miranda? Really?"

"Don't worry," Doris said, taking her books. "I've got a couple of grandnephews I'll toss her way. It's about time they started sowing their oats while they're still young enough to be considered wild. Just remember, honey," the gray-haired woman winked, "you owe me details, and I want them in inches." She held her hands to measure out such a sizeable distance that Scotti was again left gasping like a beached fish.

"Mm hm," Doris hummed sagely, and limped out of the library on gimpy legs that were fast on their way to needing a walker for support.

Scotti stared after her in absolute disbelief.

"Hey."

She jumped, snapping around to find Kurt now standing just behind her. It was everything she could do to keep her eyes on his face.

"You okay?" he asked. "Why are you jumpy?"

Somehow, she managed to shut her mouth. "Nothing. No

reason. I'm fine."

"Your shift is over, right?" He checked his wristwatch. "Not to be pushy, but we've got to go if I'm going to be to work on time."

"Uh..." Scotti said sagely. She shook her head, willing herself to snap out of it. "Right. Right, right. Just, uh... Give me a minute."

Kurt's eyebrows sank slowly down over his eyes, and he glanced from her to various parts of the library around them. "Is Gopher here?"

"Mm," Scotti quickly shook her head, her eyes falling below his belt for the barest contemplative second before she snapped her gaze away again. Her face flamed as hot as a third-degree sunburn. "No... um, just give me a minute, and I'll get my stuff."

"You look... flushed," he noted, narrowing his eyes.

Willing herself to get a grip, she pinched the bridge of her nose between thumb and forefinger, shaking her head and looking everywhere but at him. "I'm fine," she squeaked.

He stared at her a moment more, then said, "Okay, get your things together. I'll just take a quick look around."

Scotti nodded quickly, and threw herself into cleaning up her already immaculate counter area until he rounded her desk, heading out toward the parking lot. Pausing at the door to the outer hall, he turned back around.

"Hey, Scotti," he softly called. When she looked up, he measured out a distance between his hands that was even greater than Doris had. "It's this big."

He winked.

She all but died, but managed to stay on her feet. Smirking, he left the library to check the grounds, and she promptly collapsed into her chair. Burying her head in her arms, she let the flames of mortification lick all through her.

She had almost kissed him this morning, too.

And now, in the midst of all this seductive burning, that place between her legs was thumping and pulsing all over again, driving the already crazy heat inside her to burn even hotter. She didn't think she could handle much more of this.

Worse, though... when Gopher finally backed off and all

of this was over, how was she supposed to go back to normal? What if she never saw him again? What was 'normal' about that?

* * * * *

It was his first day on the job, and not only was Kurt the only pirate on the payroll in pink tights and a red and pink striped uniform shirt, but whatever laundry setting Scotti had used had shrunk the shirt three sizes. It not only fit him like a second skin, but the bottom hem stopped about two inches shy of being tucked into his pants. His midriff was showing. He looked like one of the Village People.

"Not quite the vibe we're looking for here at Pirate Pete's," Captain Tommy said when he walked in.

"Yeah," Kurt said, not quite able to stop himself from giving Scotti an accusatory stare as she slunk past him and found a quiet place to sit in the designated undersea dining area, better known as Mermaid Lagoon. "I was kind of hoping you had an extra uniform I could borrow."

"No can do, big guy," he said with a sympathetic shake of his head. "Those were the biggest I had. But... hang on, I think I've got something else that will do just as well."

Which was how on his first day of work, Kurt found himself by being promoted. He still had to wear the pink tights, but the rest of his uniform was a nice dignified black and instead of a cabin boy bussing tables, he became Pirate Pete's Birthday Boson. Not solely because he fit into what was supposed to be a baggy, loose-fitting outfit (and which absolutely was not on him), but because the existing Boson had quit earlier that morning and Kurt was the only employee Tommy could bully, force, or cajole into putting it on. It wasn't pink, that was all Kurt cared about.

Or so he thought.

And then he had his first party.

It consisted of twenty-two four-year-olds and six adults, all of which were crammed into Birthday Cove—a shallow indention of fake rocks not far from the Secret Treasure Cave play place—along with an overflow of helium inflated balloons.

The birthday boy was jumping up and down on the seat between his parents. He wore a paper pirate's hat, an eyepatch over his right eye, and was waving a plastic cutlass over his head. Although they hadn't yet cut into their Pirate Pete's grinning pirate ice cream cake, if left up to Kurt he wouldn't have given that kid any more sugar.

Of course, if left up to him, he wouldn't have been here at all. Kurt sighed. There was no help for it. He needed employment, he needed a paycheck, he needed to keep one eye on Scotti, still sitting quietly in Mermaid Lagoon, sipping on a diet soda and coloring away on the paper tablecloth with a handful of well-used Pirate Pete crayons. He didn't know if she was in full blown Little mode out there, but she'd been coloring for at least an hour now and hadn't touched her Kindle.

She was a very well-mannered Little. He wasn't used to that. Most of the Littles he'd played with in the past, both privately and at the BDSM dungeons he once frequented, they'd all been sassy, mouthy, loud, sulky and bratty. Scotti wasn't any of those things.

None of which matters, because you still can't have her.

Daddies fresh out of prison and employed in places like Pirate Pete's can't afford Littles of their own. And those who lived with their grandmothers while they tried to save up enough to afford a place of their own, did not get to be anyone's boyfriend, much less their Daddy.

Do your job, Birthday Boson.

Holding the lyrics to the birthday song in his hand, Kurt turned his back on Scotti and waded his way through all the screaming children to the table of adults. There was safety in numbers, he thought, as the kids took one look at him in his Boson get-up and went totally insane with cheering, happy glee. The pitch of their laughing, shrieking voices was deafeningly loud within the Cove.

"How old's the birthday boy?" he shouted, just to be heard over the noise.

The children almost bowled him over as they shouted back, "Four! Four! Four!"

"Four, got it!" He held up his hands to shush them all, and the room became so still and excitedly quiet as to be almost unbearable. Twenty-two children locked him the bull's-eye of their bright, grinning gazes, and they waited. He surreptitiously glanced at the lyrics one last time. He'd spent the first half hour of his shift hiding in the bathroom, trying to come up with a good excuse for why he shouldn't have to do this, and when that failed, the next half hour trying to memorize the words. Now... well, he was fairly well resigned to making a fool of himself, but while he would give in and sing the stupid song, there was absolutely no way in hell anyone could get him to do the silly dance that went with it.

Fishing his Boson's harmonica out of his pirate's coat pocket, he blew out the first musical note and drew a deep breath. To the deafening roar of twenty-two children erupting into screams of joy, he belted out,

"Oh yo ho ho!
I'm four years old
And I'm getting to be a grown-up little matey!"

As it turned out, he needn't have worried about the dancing, because each and every one of those kids did it for him, flapping their arms, shuffling their feet, and wiggling their bottoms from side to side like twenty-two little washing machines stuck in the agitation cycle. Some of them even looked kind of cute doing it, and despite himself, Kurt started to smile.

Just a little bit.

"With my pistol and my sword,
I can swing aboard
Any ship in any kingdom's navy!

But I say please and thanks,
Before I make you walk the plank,
'Cuz manners make a first class little matey!"

"You're not dancing," Captain Tommy called to him when Kurt paused to check the next lyrics.

In Mermaid Lagoon, Scotti had stopped coloring. She was standing up in her booth to see over the Cove's fake rock privacy wall, her wide and delighted gaze fixed on him singing this ridiculous song to all these sugar-high washing machines.

"Dance or walk the plank!" Captain Tommy bellowed in his 'arrrr-iest' pirate imitation, much to the kids—and Scotti's—delight.

"Oh, for fu—" Kurt sighed. He also made himself smile so he wouldn't scare anyone and danced, shuffling his feet and wiggling his hips and feeling like an absolute idiot in the middle of twenty-two ecstatic Pirate Pete wannabes.

"I've got a pirate bag,
For all my pirate swag,
And an eyepatch, and a parrot, and a peg leg.

And we get lots and lots of booty,
But we always share the looty,
'Cuz we're all a bunch of friendly, happy mateys!"

"Smile!" Captain Tommy cheerfully bellowed. Kurt smiled harder, feeling like an even bigger fool, but Tommy cheered him on anyway. "Now you're getting into the spirit of it!"

"Oh yo ho ho!
I'm four years old,
and I'm getting to be a grown-up little matey!

Yo ho ho,
Next year I'm told,
Then I'll be a grown up
With my Jolly Roger sewn up
Oh yes, then I'll be a grown up little matey!"

Although it wasn't in the script, Kurt put an impromptu stomp and 'ta-dah' wave of his arms on the end of the dance before abruptly dropping both smile and arms and trudging himself back out of Birthday Cove. Behind him, everybody erupted into cheers as Captain Tommy fired the birthday cannon, shooting a spray of glitter and confetti everywhere. Like the French fry machine, that was just one more piece of Pirate Pete equipment that he was too green and wet behind the ears to operate.

All Kurt wanted now was a chance to retire back into the breakroom long enough to gather together what tattered shreds remained of his manly pride, but Scotti's yell stopped him in his tracks.

"Captain Tommy! Oh, Captain Tommy!"

Kurt turned, his 'don't you freakin' do it' glare completely wasted on Scotti's thoroughly triggered Little.

"It's my birthday, too!" she cried out, much to the laughter of the few adults scattered throughout Mermaid Lagoon, eating late lunches or early suppers.

Kurt glared. The birthday party children cheered and instantly fled the Cove to mob her table, thrilled that they would be treated to an encore performance. Without the slightest embarrassment, Scotti hopped down to join them. Laughing, her blue eyes sparkling, she unashamedly threw herself into the pirate dance, flapping her arms and shuffling her feet with the best of them, and Captain Tommy gave him an expectant look.

"Well?" he said. "Hop to it, Birthday Boson. And this time I want to see you dancing and smiling."

He'd almost rather be unemployed.

Almost.

The way she was smiling, however, as he shuffled over to stand at her table, helped to kill his irritation. When she grinned, he had to fight to keep his glower. "I thought I told you to stay put and stay quiet."

"You did. But you just looked so cute out there, I couldn't help myself. Come on, do the pirate dance for me."

"I think I'd rather give you a good old-fashioned birthday spanking instead."

"The Birthday Boson doesn't give spankings," Captain Tommy interrupted, wheeling out the birthday cannon and pointing it straight into the air over her table. Everyone in the surrounding booths quickly moved so as not to get confetti and glitter in their food. "He sings and dances and smiles. You know, the pink tights look good on you. I think I'm going to make that a standard part of the uniform."

Kurt closed his eyes in a grimace that was just slightly longer than a blink, and then opened them again.

"I know," she smiled, and held up her finger. "That's one."

"Damn straight," he grumbled and pulled out his harmonica to begin the song anew.

The kids cheered when he was done. So did Scotti. She also threw out her arms, twirling with all the other four-year-olds as Captain Tommy shot the cannon and glitter and confetti rained gently down on her upturned face. She sat for the rest of his shift in a booth in Mermaid Lagoon, with bits of sparkle and multi-colored paper in her hair, on her clothes, and scattered all over her table and booth, swinging her feet under the table, coloring on the tablecloth and humming the birthday song under her breath.

It was all he could do not to bend over and press a kiss to her forehead each time he had to go out and bus a table after a departing customer.

A guy could fall in love with that so easily.

Not him, he mentally corrected himself. Of course not, but... someone with their life a bit more stable and together could.

Easily.

Jaw clenching twice, Kurt bussed his tables and quietly envied that faceless, unknown someone.

Chapter Eleven

"Yo ho ho, I'm four-years-old," Scotti sang, hopping out of the car now that she'd parked it in her driveway, taking her purse and the four paper tablecloths she'd completely colored in during his six-hour shift at Pirate Pete's with her. "Yo ho ho, and I'm getting to be a grown-up little matey."

Fighting back a smile, Kurt shook his head and climbed out of the car now too. She played hopscotch up her walkway cobblestones, already fishing her keys out of her purse.

"How old are you really?" he asked, trailing her to the door.

"Twenty-six," she said between puffs as she hopscotched up her three porch steps. When she reached the very top one, with an extra big hop, she spun around to flash him a grin, and in an instant became full-adult Scotti Moore as she walked up to her front door to unlock it.

Fully adult Scotti still had glitter in her hair and specks of confetti stuck to her clothes.

"And the Little side of you?" he asked, already missing her.

Shrugging one shoulder, Scotti pushed open the door and then stepped back so he could enter first. "I don't know, five or six, maybe. I never really pinned her down."

Traffic on the expressway home had been horrible. It took almost an hour to drive what would otherwise have only lasted twenty minutes. But they were home now, and the sun was down. All up and down her quiet suburban street, the streetlights were flicking on, doing limited battle with the growing darkness.

Her porch was almost completely bathed in shadows and they hadn't left any lights on inside. He made a mental note to keep the porch lit from here on out and took the lead inside. Listening for telltale signs of an intruder, he flicked on the entryway light and listened. The house remained quiet.

"What kind of Littles do you like to have?" she asked as he motioned her to come inside.

"All kinds." Closing and locking the door, he put his fingers to his lips and motioned for her to stay put. Room by room, flicking on lights and checking every window, closet and exterior door as he went, he checked to make sure they had no unwelcome vermin hiding in the shadows. Only when he was sure she was safe, did he turn the extra lights back off again and return to her at the front door. "Okay," he said, "Let's get you into pajamas, and then we'll have a quick supper before bed."

She hopped up the stairs. Literally. One step at a time, her hands on the safety railing, hopped.

"Someone had too much birthday cake," he mused, following slowly along behind her.

"I like Captain Tommy," she replied, and walked the rest of the way down the hall to the bathroom. "He's nice."

Captain Tommy was a kid, his boss and nobody that Kurt needed to instantly despise with every fiber of his being, like he suddenly found himself doing. "He gave you three pieces of cake and blew his cannon all over you twice," Kurt said, heading past her down the hall to fetch her bunny pajamas from the bedroom. "Of course, you like him."

"You didn't give me any cake or blow the cannon on me once, and I still like you," she pointed out. A few seconds later, she stuck her head out the bathroom door and called, slightly embarrassed down the hallway behind him, "That came out wrong."

Yes, it did. He didn't correct her, he just passed her pajamas through the bathroom door and then went to change out of his boson uniform. He put on a comfortable pair of sweats and a t-shirt, something he wouldn't mind sleeping in as he bedded down again on her floor, and all the while pretended that he was perfectly fine and did not have a semi-stiff 'cannon' rising to the mental image of her getting naked just down the hall from him.

He liked her too, he thought, and headed downstairs to

put both their phones on the charger. He then got the mail, answered a text from Grams when she notified him that the police had been by asking for him.

Did they have a warrant, he texted.

They did not.

Did you tell them where I am?

I did not, Grams replied, punctuating it with three frowny face emojis.

Go ahead and tell them. I'm not running from anyone. In fact, he'd welcome the chance to ask why they'd be on him this fast after one accidental run in with Krissy, and yet Scotti was sleeping in a slashed bed, and no one was even taking her seriously.

Scotti had her hair in pigtails when she came downstairs, holding onto Bat Bear by the arm. "There's a car in the driveway," she called, bringing attention to the splash of light as it brightened the tiny window in the front door.

"Get down," he told her, jogging back out of the kitchen toward the front door again.

She dropped and sat on the stairs, watching as he peeked outside.

"Dominos," he said, reading the brightly lit sign across the top of the car.

"Woot!" she said and scrambled back up again. "Pizza's here."

"When the hell did you order a pizza?" he called as she scrambled up the stairs to fetch her purse again.

"When you were checking the house," she answered. "I was hungry. I hope you like Hawaiian and mushrooms."

His exasperated sigh was cut short by the ringing of the doorbell. If it weren't for the fact that she was cute, cheerful, spritely, and growing on him, he'd be tempted to throttle her for bringing someone to the house without warning him first.

"I love Hawaiian," he muttered to no one in particular.

Scotti came running back down the stairs with her wallet in hand, and he stood by, waiting while she paid the delivery driver. Closing the door, she ignored his censuring frown and carried the pizza and a two-liter bottle of pop past him to the dining room.

"Yo ho ho," she sang under her breath, pigtails swinging, and dropped her load on the table.

"Plates," he said as she opened the box.

"Pizza boxes are plates you don't have to wash," she replied and pulled out a hot slice. She was eating on it before he crossed the threshold from the dining room to the kitchen. He got two plates and two cups and returned just as she was sitting down, humming and chewing and swinging her feet.

"So," she said, before taking another bite. "Do you miss being a cop?"

"Don't talk with your mouth full," he told her, distributing the plates and laying hers under her hands, whether she wanted to use it or not. "And yes, sometimes I do."

"I bet you were good at it," she said, between chews. "Plus, you know… handcuffs."

He almost fumbled the two-liter, laughing instead of opening it. "Police issue handcuffs are not to be used in the bedroom," he told her, only semi-sternly and poured them both some pop. Fortunately, he noticed the label before he killed his tastebuds on the first sip. "You got diet?"

"I'm wassing my fig-ur," she said, sucking air around a mouthful of hot cheese and pineapple.

That made two of them. He'd been watching her figure pretty much all day. Of course, he hadn't yet found anything wrong with it, but he kept that particular observation to himself and helped himself to water from the tap.

"All right," he said, selecting a hot slice of pizza from the box. "You know my sad story. Tell me all about you and the groundhog."

"Mm," she gave a rueful chuckle, sucking tomato sauce off her thumb. "What's to tell? I was young, he was there, it was good for a while and then it was over. And, actually, I even knew it was over before I knew about the affair. All that did was help me get my head right about packing up and leaving."

They ate for a while in silence. She had two slices of the Hawaiian pizza, and he ate the rest. To be fair, he left the last piece sitting in the box, politely giving her a chance to claim it for herself right up until she started humming that pirate birthday song again. He finished off the pizza with a clear conscience after that.

"Knock it off," he told her.

"What?"

"I have to sing that at work, I don't want to listen to it at home."

"It's a catchy song." She kept humming it.

"You know, I never did give you that birthday spanking," Kurt said aloud. "Do you suppose it's too late?"

"It wasn't really my birthday," she said, chuckling. "You just looked so cute out there, singing and dancing and absolutely hating it."

And then not only was she humming, but she was doing the Boson shuffle, sitting there in her chair with her blue eyes sparkling with amusement. "Yo ho ho, we're all happy, friendly mateys."

She let out a laughing squeak when he abruptly pushed back his chair and even tried to dive for safety, but he caught the back of her pajamas anyway. Her squeak became a shriek as he lifted her out of her seat and dumped her without preamble across his waiting lap.

He really liked these pajamas. That Velcro bottom flap made everything so convenient, although it was something of a surprise to find she wasn't wearing panties underneath it tonight.

She must have been a bit startled too. From the moment he ripped the Velcro tabs apart, baring her bottom to the dining room lights and his open palm, she stopped laughing. She also stopped struggling. Holding onto his leg with one hand and the chair he was sitting on with her other, she twisted back far enough to see him, and for him to see the soft pink blush she wore. The one that didn't have anything to do with mortification because she was in trouble, but which had everything to do with being bent across his knee, with her bare ass on display and his open hand ready to deliver what in his head he knew was going to be anything but stern discipline.

"Are you having fun," he asked, "pushing Daddy's buttons like this?"

"No," she squeaked, biting her bottom lip and shaking her head. But he could see her timid smile hiding in the way she chewed her lip. She wasn't at all scared of him, and he liked that.

"Are you going to keep driving me crazy?"

"I promise to try my level best not to?" she replied, her hesitant voice lilting into a question, which as far as he was concerned, was submissive code for: Please, by all means, spank me.

So Kurt did, but not like either time before. This wasn't a punishment; he didn't start off hard and only get harder. Instead, he started off soft, with swats that hardly qualified as such, with plenty of rubbing, squeezing and cupping the malleable flesh of her bottom with his hand in between.

She had a fantastic ass. Perfect for spanking. Round and wobbly when he smacked it, firm and soft when he caressed. And she liked it. She liked it so much, she relaxed across his lap and titled back her hips to offer up her bottom for more. The little sound she made in the back of her throat was the kind of sound he'd happily have ripped her clothes off to... followed by his own. But no, he wasn't going to have sex with her, he told himself. That wasn't what this was about.

This was about showing her the Daddy wasn't always a hard-ass disciplinarian. It was about showing her, he had a sense of humor. That he knew how to play with her inner Little. Knew how to satisfy her, no matter what she was needing, when or even how often she needed it.

His slow spanks picked up both speed and force. His gentle, squeezing caresses came less often. He was giving her two—three—five brisk swats at a time now, before pausing to rub, and her hand against his legs became a fist, clinging to the soft, excess cloth of his sweats.

Don't do it, he told himself.

But already his hand was moving, off the full summit of her softly blushing bottom and down into the valley between her legs where the cloth of her pajamas kept things hidden in shadow. At the first touch of his fingers caressing a request for access along the inner slopes of her thighs, she granted it, parting her legs for him without hesitation. She did let go of the chair though, and grabbed onto his sweatpants with both fists now. Her breathing was soft, but shaky, and when his fingers dipped into moisture gathering along the folds of her heated pussy, the sigh she exhaled could have doubled as a moan.

Smooth. She was absolutely smooth, the plump flesh of her outer lips as soft as the name he gave her as his fingers slipped between her folds in search of the pleasuring nub he very quickly found. "I think it's time these pajamas come down, babygirl. What do you think?"

If she shook her head—if she hesitated in the slightest—he told himself, he would take that as a no and respect it. He wasn't a man who forced, and he didn't want to hurt her by taking advantage.

She didn't hesitate and she definitely did not shake her head. Pushing up off his lap, she climbed to her feet with all the unsteadiness of a woman already sinking into the haze of arousal and, blushing furiously, she unzipped the front of her bunny pajamas. The only thing beneath was the soft paleness of her naked skin.

She unwrapped herself to him as if she were a present, or maybe he only thought that because watching her bare herself began to feel like Christmas morning. Shoulders first, as she shyly shrugged her arms out of her sleeves, then shimmying her pajamas down off her hips and then her legs, until finally she stepped out of them. And there she was. Lean and slender, with small, pert breasts, trim belly and hips, and an ass that could have stopped traffic. Librarian, hell. She could have been a movie star. So long as he was the only one who got to see her like this, she could be his movie star all day and all night long.

He patted his knee and she obediently lay herself back over his lap.

"Are you a Little who likes having your bottom spanked?" he asked, letting his hand wander the surface of each round buttock in turn. "No, ma'am," he said, when she tensed and eventually, she made herself relax again.

"If I'm not in trouble."

"You're definitely not in trouble," he promised, adjusting her so her bottom was positioned more prominently. He tapped the backs of her legs. "Open. Show Daddy what's his."

Her hands fisted against his leg and she tensed all over again, but after a moment, she also moved her feet apart, opening up her legs, and putting every secret inch of herself on blatant display.

The lips of her pussy shone wet under the recessed dining room lights. She was plump and pink with arousal, and he could just see the tip of her clit peeking out from beneath its hood as if every bit as shy for attention as Scotti was.

Every inch of her was about to get all the attention she ached for, but first...

His open hand came down with a clap that sounded harder than it actually was. He knew, because although she jolted at the impact, her eyes also closed, her breath became a wanton sigh, and her head lowered. He spanked her slow, but steady, painting her bottom pink, taking his cues from every wiggling squirm as to when to smack harder or softer, faster or slower, and when to switch targets completely, laying a single swat full across her hot little pussy.

Compared to the force he laid upon her bottom, the slap he gave her pussy was gentle, but she still jumped and cried out, a lusty shout that was quickly followed by a low-throated moan and a grind of her hips against his knee. She shivered, the flesh of her bottom clenching, and when he pulled his hand back, his fingers came away wet and fragrant with the scent of her arousal.

He was not immune to that scent, that sight, and certainly not to the squirming feel of her grinding upon his thigh. The thrum of arousal pulsed through his veins, burning him from the inside out, pulsing in his head and his chest, and absolutely in his cock. Already he was hard as hell, prodding up against her belly, begging to go where his fingers couldn't help but return to wander again and again, slipping into wetness, circling the sensitive tip of her clit, rolling it until she was mewling whimpers and rolling her hips along with him.

Her legs began to shake. Her tiny toes were curled.

"Say Daddy, may I come please," he told her, catching her clit between his fingers and flicking it with his thumb. Slow flicks made her back arch and turned her breathy moans erratic. Fast flicks made her legs snap shut and her gorgeous ass hump up and down, riding his hand in a way that made his cock instantly jealous. "Say it. Daddy, may I come please."

"D-Daddy," she broke off with a moan. She gripped and re-gripped at his pants, her trembling thighs spreading open wide. He wondered if she even knew she was doing it, granting him better access, filling every breath he took with the erotic aroma of her. He loved her bucking, grinding, increasingly desperate gasps. He loved even more that he only gave her one line to repeat and yet she had to cover her face with both hands before she could plead out, "Daddy, m-may I come? Please, Daddy!"

She got it out just in time too. Already her bottom was tightening, her hips jerking. He barely got two fingers up inside her in time to feel those telltale convulsions as her orgasm ripped through her and her greedy pussy clamped down on the digits he pumped in and out of her. She was soft, slick, molten.

Heaven.

She was heaven, perfection, and he didn't stop fucking her with his hand until he'd wrung every last convulsive twitch from her bucking hips.

His turn.

Her legs were like jello. He had to support her, even just for the short time it took to pick her up off his lap and bend her over the dining room table. Had they not already eaten all the pizza, it would have been on the floor where he sent the box flying when he slapped it out of the way. He didn't bother undressing. Who the hell had time for that? Shoving his pants down out of the way, he grabbed the back of her hair and slammed up into her like, well... a man who'd been in prison for two years.

Her cry was all pleasure with only the slightest twinge of guttural discomfort—if discomfort it could even be called. She was tight; but she took him. Every inch. He made sure of it. Over and over again, he thrust hard and he thrust deep, and he didn't stop. Not until they were both shaking, both coming, both crying out, and in a rush of hot ecstasy that he felt pulling all the way down through his balls, he drained every drop of fluid he had into the beautiful heat of her.

She collapsed, limp and panting, still bent over the table.
She was still perfection. She was still heaven.
And he wasn't just thinking that because she was the first

woman he'd been with since Dana.

She deserved a hell of a lot better than a thirty-two-year-old ex-cop turned Birthday Boson for a fast food restaurant where he wasn't even qualified to operate the fry machine.

He pulled out of her body with no small reluctance.

He never should have taken this job. He never should have had her call him Daddy. She was his now. How in the world was he ever going to let her go?

Running his fingers through her golden hair, he pulled her head back far enough to kiss the top of her bangs, and then he pushed off both her and the table. "Come on, babygirl."

On wobbly legs, she followed him to the bathroom. He cleaned her up. No condom, damn it. Automatically, the potential consequences of his actions doubled in his head. Tripled. What the hell was wrong with him?

She leaned up against the sink while he washed the stain of him from out between her legs. Drowsy as she was, she smiled the whole time as he helped her back into her pajamas. That smile killed him; his will crumbled.

Just one night. It was okay to have one night. Tomorrow, they'd talk about it, put things back to rights. He'd do what he should have done when she first approached him about this job and he saw her bed cut to shreds—he'd call every friend he used to have at the station and see if any of them still cared enough about him to do him a solid. He'd pass her over into their care and he'd bow out, because while physically, mentally, and sexually he could love her, take care of her, and protect her, he couldn't do a damn thing for her financially. He was a felon. That stigma would follow him for the rest of his life. He didn't have a home of his own anymore. He didn't have a car. He couldn't buy her coloring book or a stuffed animal, or even an ice cream cone.

He couldn't be a Daddy in the way he wanted to be, and that she deserved to have him be.

He was pretty well useless to her.

So yeah, tomorrow was soon enough to admit all that out loud to her. For tonight, though... tonight he could still pretend. And since they were pretending, it was perfectly okay for him to lower himself onto one knee, lean forward and kiss the soft, bare skin of her mons, where the smell of him still mingled with hers.

"Let's go upstairs," he said. "Daddy's going to kiss you in special places, and he wants you one more time before we go to sleep."

Slipping her fingers through his short, dark hair, she nodded. Her desire was naked in her eyes when he took her hand and he loved that she fell so sweetly into step alongside him, letting herself be led from the bathroom.

Which was as far as he got before he felt the whisper of a breeze that did not belong in a house where all the doors were locked and the windows were bolted.

The front door was standing wide open. Every hair on the back of his neck stood straight up on end when he saw it, but he never had a chance to react.

In retrospect, getting clubbed over the back of the head by Gopher was just what he deserved for allowing himself to have something he shouldn't and for being more concerned about 'pretending' than in keeping Scotti safe. And contrary to popular belief, his world did not go instantly black just before he hit the floor. It exploded into stars first.

Chapter Twelve

Kurt came to lying on his back in the hallway between the bathroom and the stairs with a warm, comfortable, coconut-scented lump lying on top of him: Scotti, grunting softly as she wriggled back and forth on his chest.

He took a deep breath of her, a slow smile drawing across his lips as he felt the heat of her hips squirming over his, the pillowy softness of her breasts mashed against him, and the tickling caress of her hair against his neck and cheek. Not yet awake enough to wonder how they'd got this way, he was still a red-blooded convict fresh out of prison, and he didn't need awareness to have a red-blooded physical reaction to the nearness of a very attractive woman

"Oh, wow," Scotti said and abruptly stopped wriggling. She drew back a few inches to look down between them, no doubt at the erection rising up to prod at her. "Oh... oh, wow!"

He smiled. "Good morning, beautiful."

Glancing up at him now, her eyes were as wide as dinner plates. "Kurt?"

"Want to get frisky before work?" He wiggled his eyebrows.

"Seriously?" she asked, not looking the slightest bit amorous. "Snap out of it or I'm going to hit you, and it won't be in the head!"

It wasn't until he moved to hold her that he became aware of something being wrong. There was an uncomfortable lump under the small of his back. His hands, he suddenly realized, were tied tightly at the wrist. And he'd been lying on them for quite a while, because not only were his fingers numb beyond the point of tingling, but fire-hot agony stabbed up through his shoulders when he tried to move his arms. That's when it all came flooding back to him.

"Oh, hell," he groaned, closing his eyes again. "Where's Gopher?"

"Finally, you get my name right."

Heavy clumping footsteps came into the dining room from the kitchen, and Kurt opened his eyes in time to see Scotti's ex, a butcher's cleaver dangling from one hand, crossing the floor to them. Dark hair, dark eyes, tall and lean as a scarecrow, he started down the hallway toward them.

Scotti froze, flinching when she saw what he carried, but Gopher wasn't looking at her. His jealous stare was locked on Kurt, and he continued to adjust his grip on the cleaver even as he circled all the way around them once before stopping above his head. Kurt had to tip his head back to look up at him. Which put him right at eyeball level with the tip of the cleaver when Gopher hunkered down, arms draped over his knees, to look at him.

"You," Gopher said, tipping his head and finally looking at Scottie, "promised faithfulness and loyalty when you signed yourself over into my care as your dominant."

Kurt could feel her slight trembling, but it did not show in her voice when she replied, "You were supposed to be loyal too, but you had an affair."

"That doesn't mean I loved her."

"You threatened to kill me when I said we were over. You have threatened me so many times no one believes me when I tell them anymore. You slashed my bed with your knife."

"That doesn't mean I don't love you," he cautioned.

"Gopher." Scotti grunted softly as she tried to rise up far enough to meet his eyes instead of his knife. "It's over. I don't love you anymore. Not like a devoted submissive should love her Dom. Please get it through your head, because we're done."

The cleaver wavered as Gopher gripped and re-gripped the handle, and Kurt had to turn his head to one side as the blade dropped an inch, almost close enough to touch his forehead.

"Uh, Scottie," he said, not entirely sure if bringing Gopher's attention back to him was a good idea right now, but... "Ix-nay on the ear-Day ohn-Jay."

Jaw clenching, Gopher shifted his angry stare back to him. "Would you like to be on the top or bottom?"

"Of?" Kurt asked, fairly certain that he wasn't going to like the answer.

"The shallow unmarked grave I've been digging in the backyard." Gopher stood. "Excuse me, I need to get back to work if I want to be all cleaned up by dawn. Call me when you've made your decision, will you?"

He turned and walked back to the kitchen, and a moment later Kurt heard the sliding glass door open. "He's really very polite for a man named Gopher."

"He's also a very fast digger," Scotti said, throwing herself back into her warmish wriggles against her bonds.

"How are we connected?"

"Around the waist, but only once," she panted. "He didn't have enough rope."

"I feel it now." Ignoring the pain in his shoulders, he lifted his hips, trying to get his bound wrists under his butt. He stopped when she said, "Hang on, don't do that."

He lay still, listening to her soft pants of pain as she strained.

"He may be a fast digger," Scotti puffed. "But he's not very good at tying knots. Ow!" she whispered, but just as suddenly, her hands were free. She shimmied right out of the single twist of rope that circled their middles, sliding off his stomach and down between his legs, and damn if his cock simply was not getting the message about their being in a life-threatening situation right now.

"Roll," she said, helping to heave him onto his side despite the pain that lanced his shoulder. She bit the knot to get it loosened, and in two quick yanks of the rope, he was free.

He sat up, hissing and rubbing his wrists as the circulation rushed back into his hands and aching shoulders. She had to help him shrug out of the phone cord because his hands refused to work right away, but the minute he was back on his feet, he hooked his arm around her and whispered, "Grab the rope."

He patted through his pockets, finding wallet, keys—Gopher hadn't even bothered to rob him—and, bingo, his cellphone. Scrambling as far as the doorway to the dining room, he peeked through to the kitchen, but he couldn't see the sliding glass doors much less Gopher from here. He could, however, just make out the metallic chink of a shovel head stabbing into dirt and rocks.

"Where's Gopher?" Scotti whispered.

"Still digging," Kurt said, tapping his phone on and flipping open to his most recent contacts. He wasted no time calling. "Hey, mother fucker," he said, before the DA could even say hello. "You want my ass? You come and get it." He gave Scotti's address, rattling it off twice, just in case. "Also, I'd appreciate it if you hurried, because there's about to be a murder."

"What?" Emerson Davis said, the only word he was able to get out before Kurt hung up the phone.

His second call was to 911, at which point he didn't bother saying anything. He just stuck the phone in his pocket and let it run so they could trace it.

He grabbed Scotti's arm and pulled her down the hallway, away from the dining room toward the living room. "Do you know any of your neighbors?"

"If you think I'm leaving you here, you're out of your mind," she said, in anything but her Little voice.

"What makes you think I'm not going to run too?" Which was when he turned and saw the front door. It wasn't yawning open anymore. Gopher had closed it. He'd also nailed a two-by-four across the threshold, preventing their easy escape. "Son of a—"

Why couldn't he hear digging anymore?

Holding up a silencing hand when Scotti opened her mouth, he was still listening intently when the sliding glass door slid open again.

Grabbing her arm, he hurried her upstairs as quickly and quietly as he could. They were halfway down the hall, when he heard Gopher sigh.

"You're only making me wish I'd cut your head off when I had the chance," he called out. The front closet door opened, then closed. "You're also pissing me off," Gopher said. "There's only so many hiding places in this house."

Pushing Scotti down the hall ahead of him, Kurt stopped at each door—the spare room, the bathroom and finally, her bedroom—pressing the lock on each one and closing the doors behind him.

"That won't confuse him for long," he whispered, as soon as they were locked in her bedroom together. He went to the window next, throwing it open as wide as it would go. He stuck his head out, leaning well out over the eave of the decorative roof that shielded the window directly below them. There was only about two feet of shingle space to stand on, and he didn't like the slant. Still, beggars could hardly be choosy at times like this. "Out you go," he said, ducking back inside and reaching for her arm.

She folded them across her chest and shook her head.

"We are in serious trouble," he told her. "Pick a neighbor you trust, get them to call the cops. They might have your address flagged as a troublemaker, but I guarantee if they get two calls from this street, they will send police."

She shook her head, but for all that she might not want to leave him, her expression was already waffling.

"I can move faster and make decisions better if you're not with me," he said, giving her shoulders a gentle shake, "and if I know you're safe."

That convinced her, but reluctantly. He helped her crawl out onto the roof, and held her steady while she leaned out over the edge.

"Do you see him?" he whispered.

She shook her head, and they both jumped when they heard the loud bang of a door being kicked in down the hall. Wood splintered, and Gopher called, "Come out, come out, wherever you are."

He was at the spare room. He would be at the bathroom next, and they were running out of time.

"I'm going to lower you as far as I can, then I'm going to drop you and you're going to run," he told her. She shook her head again, but stopped when he said, "Yes, you are. Tuck and roll, babygirl."

Holding onto the windowsill for his own balance, he took firm hold of her wrist while she got down on her belly and slowly lowered herself over the edge. She squeaked and grabbed his hand with both of hers when gravity pulled her down, but Kurt held on and didn't let her fall. He lowered her as far over the edge as he could reach.

"Ready?" he whispered.

One of her hands let go. Just before he let her drop, down the hall, the bathroom door was kicked in.

"I've got you now, motherfucker," Gopher said, his voice growing louder as he came down the hallway to Scotti's bedroom.

Kurt crawled out the window, but he didn't go down. He didn't know how late it was, but it was dark. In the glow of the evenly spaced streetlamps, he caught a glimpse of Scotti in her pink bunny pajamas racing across the road to the neighbor across the street. Unlike the neighbors to either side of them, that house still had lights on.

It took two kicks for Gopher to break through Scotti's bedroom door, and Kurt made sure Gopher caught sight of his dangling legs a half second before he pulled himself up onto the roof.

"You fucking monkey," Gopher mused, leaning out the window after him.

Kurt ran along the edge, looking for an escape route. He found one almost directly opposite of the way he'd come up.

Gopher knew where he was heading almost before he did. When Kurt dropped onto the back-porch roof one story below, he only just caught a glimpse of the other man's shadow racing past the bathroom window, heading back downstairs. Lowering himself off that roof next had Kurt dropping into Scotti's azaleas. He stumbled over the decorative rocks that ringed her flowerbed and promptly fell right into his own impromptu grave. It was so dark he hadn't even seen the hole until he hit the bottom of it. It wasn't even; it wasn't even deep.

"Half-ass idiot," he said, scrambling to his feet just as his opponent ran out of the house through the sliding glass door. "I thought Gophers could dig!"

Gopher launched himself over the deck railing, tackling him back into the bottom of the grave. Kurt was bigger and stronger, but Gopher was faster. He was also driven, and it took every ounce of strength Kurt had to kick, thrash and wrestle his way to the top of their two-dog dog pile.

Gopher grabbed him by the throat. Unable to pry himself loose, Kurt grabbed him the same way. The wrestling match became a choke-off, and just as Gopher was gasping, wheezing, and starting to loosen his grip, stars exploded through Kurt's head once more. A shower of dirt, flowers and broken pottery shards from the clay pot that had hit the back of his head rained down over Gopher's at-once both dazed and surprised face.

Vaguely, Kurt heard Scotti's startled, "Oh no!" just before, for the second time that night, Kurt slumped unconscious.

* * * * *

"You both are very lucky that I got here when I did," District Attorney Emerson Davis told Scotti and Kurt, as they sat side by side on her front porch steps.

Hunkered in front of Kurt, an ambulance medic ran a finger back and forth, making him track it as a way of checking his responses. Scotti had never felt more guilty as she watched that, or more relieved when the medic said, "I don't think there's any serious damage, but I do recommend you go to the hospital, just to be sure."

"I'm fine," Kurt grumbled, shifting the cold pack over the massive goose egg her pot had left on the back of his head. In the dark, he'd looked like Gopher. She'd thought he was Gopher, and she'd just reacted, grabbing the first heavy thing she could find.

She could have hurt him.

She had hurt him; she could have killed him.

Holding one of his hands in both of hers, she rubbed his fingers and felt quietly horrible while several police officers tromped out of her house, leading a handcuffed Gopher past her down the steps to the three patrol cars now blocking the end of her driveway. Their flashing red, blue and white lights splashed her house, her lawn, the entire street. Every house she could see had neighbors standing on their porch, watching and talking amongst themselves.

"You're very lucky," the DA said again as Gopher was put into the back of a patrol car. "I'd hate to think what might have happened if I hadn't recognized who was calling me a motherfucker."

"Thank you," Scotti told him, sincerely.

Adjusting the cold pack again, Kurt didn't even look up.

"You really should go to the hospital," the EMT tried again, packing up his kit to leave.

"I don't need the bill or the hassle," Kurt muttered.

"I'll take him," Scotti promised.

He looked at her. It was not a happy look. Also, she recognized stubborn when she saw it, but she was smart enough to know she had a better chance of badgering him into seeing a doctor if she waited until they were alone.

Exchanging identical looks, the EMTs went back to their truck, loaded up their gear and shut off the flashing amber lights. Then they drove away.

The police were also leaving.

"We'll need you both to come down to the station," Davis said before turning to her. "I'm going to put you in touch with our domestic violence agency, okay? We'll need a full statement of what happened, but considering the state of the house, the bed you showed us, and the hole in the backyard, I don't think you need to worry that Gopher will be released from jail any time soon."

"Thanks," Scotti managed a smile for his sake, rubbing at Kurt's fingers, trapped between her nervous hands.

"You guys have had a busy night." Turning to Kurt, the DA said, "How about you call me in the morning and we'll set up a time so you can come down and talk to me?"

"How about you stop beating around the bush and just do it?" Kurt replied, calm and even, and seeming only mildly irritated until he pinned the other man with a hard stare. It was like that first day at the library all over again, standing in the bathroom with a man who stood before her as stiff and as emotionless as a marble statue. Only this time the statue was sitting, and he wasn't quite as expressionless as he used to be. Or maybe she could just read him a bit better now.

"What do you mean?" Davis asked.

"Arrest me," Kurt said bluntly. "It's what you've been hounding after me for, isn't it?"

"No."

"So just do it al—" Kurt stopped, blinking. "What do you mean, no?"

Slipping his hands into his pockets, the DA drew a deep breath. "I've been trying for the last twenty-four hours to figure out how to say this to you, and I still don't have the words. So I'm just going to say it. Krissy Degrassi walked into the station on Philmont and Fifth yesterday and turned herself in. Claims she framed a man because she felt threatened because of his relationship with her mother. Seems that man was a cop. Seems he went to jail for two years because the overeager DA who tried his case was more interested in proving he could do his job, so he didn't look too hard at all the little inconsistencies."

Scotti looked down at Kurt's hand she was holding. His fingers had tightened on hers. She wasn't even sure he knew he was doing it.

"What are you saying to me?" Kurt asked, evenly.

Pushing his hands that much deeper into his pockets, the DA said, "I'm saying that when you come to my office tomorrow, there is a package on my desk for you. It has your reinstatement papers in it, along with your badge and a check for lost wages—all the back pay, vacation time, and sick days. I understand the City is already consulting over an appropriate settlement offer."

"*What*," Kurt asked again, slightly more perplexed now, "are you saying to me?"

Sighing, the DA hung his head a moment, and when he finally straightened up again, he said, "Call my office when you're ready. Maybe by then, I'll have figured out how better to apologize for my part in ruining your life. So…" Nodding, he walked away to his car, parked a short way down the street.

"I got my badge back," Kurt said, stunned. Taking the cold pack off his head, he looked at it and then at her. "I also got hit in the head with a potful of begonias."

"Daisies," she said, somewhat sheepishly. "It was an accident. I was aiming for Gopher. Are you…" She rubbed his hand between hers. "Are you m-mad at me?"

He squeezed her hand. "No, I'm not mad," he sighed.

"Because I would understand if you were," she rushed to assure him. "I mean, I think I broke like all your rules tonight and..."

He held up his finger. "One rule."

"The most important rule," she pressed, even as she wondered why. She looked down at her hands, wrapped so tight around his, as if she were afraid to let him go.

Because she *was* afraid, she suddenly realized. She was afraid to let go of his hand because Gopher was caught now. He was going to go to prison, and she no longer needed a bodyguard.

He had no more reason to stay.

"I guess you don't need my paycheck anymore," she said, hearing the words and knowing they were hers, but her lips felt numb. It was like someone else saying them.

"No, I do not." He squeezed her hand again. "Also, I got my badge back, backpay for the time I spent in prison, plus the time I spent waiting for trial. I can afford to get my own place now."

He tipped his head, looking at her sideways. A corner of his mouth lilted into a smile that made her stomach flipflop in all the best and the worst ways. Because now she was going to lose him. She was going to lose her Daddy.

"I can buy a car," he said, followed by, "I can go back to work at a place where operating the fry machine is not my sole and overwhelming goal for the future."

She tried to laugh. Hating herself for being so self-absorbed that she felt worse for herself right now than she felt happy for him. A less self-absorbed person would not have picked that moment to say, "You don't have to be my Daddy anymore now, either."

"No, I do not," he agreed, with a cheerfulness that stabbed her in the stomach as if with a hundred razor-sharpened knives, right up until he said, "Now I get to be your Daddy for no other reason than because we both want me to be."

His hand squeezed hers back, two quick pulses of comfort that shot through her like lightning. Lightning that hit her in weirdly erotic places. Behind her knees, the insides of her thighs. That spot on her mons where he had stopped to kiss her just before Gopher broke into the house.

God, the tips of her nipples. They were budding so hard for him right now all she could feel was how erotic it felt just to breathe. With every in- and exhale, they scraped the inside of her pajamas like a bra made of steel wool.

"I can buy you coloring books," he said shifting on the step to face her now. "I can buy you an ice cream cone."

"I could have bought my own ice cream cone," she said, her voice quavering wildly. God, was she about to cry? She was. Her eyes were swimming, filling rapidly with tears. Oh, and great, now her nose was running. She sniffled. "I can buy my own coloring books, too. I don't need that."

"That's not the point."

She shook her head, lost now because she thought she knew what he was saying, but maybe she was wrong. "What is the point?"

"Scotti..." He took both her hands in his, holding them. "Do you want me to be your Daddy, without pay and for longer than six weeks?"

She burst into tears. She didn't mean to, it just happened. She also threw her arms around his neck and crawled into his lap so he could hold her, all of her, and she didn't care how many neighbors were milling around outside watching them.

"Yes!" she whispered into the side of his neck. "Yes, Daddy, please! I thought you were mad at me. I thought you were going to leave."

His arms tightened around her, holding her as close as two people could come.

"Of course, I'm mad at you," he said fondly. "You hit me with a flower pot. I'm going to make a new rule about that. I'm also going to make a new rule about humming or singing anything that came from Pirate Pete's. Or doing Daddy's laundry, but frankly, we've got more important things to discuss right now."

Tipping back her head, she met his smile with one of her own. "Like what?"

"We still have things to do before we go to sleep tonight."

She drew back a little further, brow furrowing. "Like what?" she asked again.

He remained quiet, his gaze slowly heating, waiting for her to remember. And she did. The memory hit her clit first, before zinging out through all the rest of her. He wanted to kiss her special place and have her one more time.

"B-but you're hurt," she protested, her face and belly both flushing hot with a slow, molten flowing sensation that wasted no time in spilling down between her legs.

"I'm a guy, I just got out of prison, and I am not that hurt." *Bed*, he mouthed and smacked her on the butt.

It didn't hurt, but she hopped up off his lap and he came hopping up right after her. He chased her into the house and up the stairs, smacking her butt every step of the way until, by the time she reached her bedroom, she was breathless from laughter and running, but most of all, from excitement.

He took his t-shirt off over his head, dropping it on the floor as he pursued her, slowly now, all the way to the edge of the bed. "I get to unwrap the present this time," he said, pushing her hands away from her pajama zipper. She understood what that meant, but she liked that he took his own sweet time unzipping her. He peeled her out of her clothes slowly, kissing and caressing the parts of her as he bared them. Her shoulders, breasts, belly, thighs. He even kissed her feet before stripping her completely bare and laying her down on the bed.

None of those were her special place, though. That he found on the journey back up her and from the moment his hot mouth made contact, nothing else mattered.

It was just her, and him, and the sighing moans he wrought from her one kiss, one nibble, and eventually, one slow, deep thrust at a time.

Just her, and him.

Forever.

The End

Be the first to get information on free stories, new releases, giveaways and prizes? Join my newsletter! http://MarenSmith.com/newsletter/

Follow me on Bookbub for the latest in sales and special release prices!

For other books by Maren Smith, visit her page on Amazon.

Made in the USA
Columbia, SC
08 July 2021